Hickory Dickory

Edited by Liz Thornbury

New
Fiction

New Fiction

First published in Great Britain in 2006 by:
New Fiction
Remus House
Coltsfoot Drive
Peterborough
PE2 9JX
Telephone: 01733 898102
Website: www.forwardpress.co.uk

All Rights Reserved

© Copyright Contributors 2006

SB ISBN 1 85929 142 2

Foreword

When 'New Fiction' ceased publishing there was much wailing and gnashing of teeth, the showcase for the short story had offered an opportunity for practitioners of the craft to demonstrate their talent.

Phoenix-like from the ashes, 'New Fiction' has risen with the sole purpose of bringing forth new and exciting short stories from new and exciting writers.

The art of the short story writer has been practised from ancient days, with many gifted writers producing small, but hauntingly memorable stories that linger in the imagination.

I believe this selection of stories will leave echoes in your mind for many days. Read on and enjoy the pleasure of that most perfect form of literature, the short story.

Parvus Est Bellus.

Contents

The Pidgeon Man	Barbara Dunning	1
Arthur And The X-Ray Machine	Peter Asher	6
Little Davey And The Magical Fruit	Stuart Brierley	13
A Winter's Tale	Ariana Luisa Chiarelli	15
Golden Mermaid	Jenifer Ellen Austin	17
Jo Jo	David R Morgan	22
Loafer The Beagle	Gerard Allardyce	24
The Wallabies In The Tree House	Barbara Russell	28
Sidney The Brain Cell And The Amazing Drop	Linda Knight	31
Annabelle's Cloud Nine	Hazel Brydon	36
Aimée And Jack In London	Janet Granger	41
Katie And The Little Owl Return To The Magical Wood	Christine Hardemon	44
The Dragon's Tale	Emma Lockyer	49
Findel's Apprentice - Elves And Dragons	Josephine Carter	52
Stolen Dragen	Sam Denniss	56
Lucy And Her Unusual Pet	C M A Hughes	61
A Little Star In The Snow	Rosemary Yvonne Vandeldt	64
Greed	Reana Beauly	67
The Rainbow's End	Bryony Freeman	70
A Summer's Day In Derrybeg	Ellen Spiring	71
The Three Elephants	Alan Hardy	75
Daisy Duckling	A R Carter	79
A Narrow Squeak	Avis E Wolfenden	81
Castle Of The Night	Glenwyn Peter Evans	83
The Wish Fairy	Susan Mary Robertson	88
On Top Of The World	Opal Innsbruk	90
Special	S Mullinger	95
Next-Door's Cat	Ivy Allpress	100
A Day In Gracie's Garden	Peggy Finch	102
Arachnid And Me On Our Initial Space Journey	Maureen Dawson	104
The Ghosts Of Christmas Past	Neil Wesson	107

The Mystery Of The Missing Necklace	Angela Bradley	110
Norman Meets The Googliebird	Michelle Hinton	114
The Belly Button Bears	Susannah Walker	119

The Stories

The Pigeon Man

Barbara Dunning

Ernest opened his front door and peered out of his little terraced house. He shivered as an icy blast of wind met him. Picking up the shabby black leather bag and turning up his collar he stepped out into the greyness of a February day. Locking the faded green door behind him, he trudged down Hope Street as he did every morning, taking care not to trip on the accumulated rubbish. 'Hope Street' - what a name! There were discarded chip papers and pop cans everywhere. Paint was peeling from the doors of the long dreary row of terraced houses. Graffiti disfigured many walls, and gates creaked on broken hinges.

Apart from a thin, miserable mongrel, Ernest was the only living being in the street that day. The cruel wind lashed at him and ripped an out of date poster from its hoarding.

'I'm coming my little friends,' the old man muttered to himself as he clutched his worn grey overcoat closer to him, and battled with the weather.

At the corner, he paused a moment to get his breath, then carefully he crossed the main road, and walked in the shelter provided by a row of shops. The light from the windows cheered him a little and he quickened his step for he was later than usual. His feathered friends would be waiting for him.

Twenty minutes later and gasping for breath, he turned in at the big iron gates of the park.

As soon as he did so there was the sound of rushing wings and in no time at all, he was surrounded by pigeons. Grey ones, white ones, brown ones, all flocked around him.

'Hello my little ones,' he panted, 'I'm sorry I'm late.'

Opening the black bag he threw the food to them, talking all the while. 'Come Joey, get your share. Percy, don't be so greedy, leave some for Ben.' The bag was soon empty. He closed the zip. 'See you tomorrow.'

Ernest turned to go. As he did so, another fierce gust of wind caught him full in the face. He gasped, clutched his chest, and with a moan, slipped unconscious to the ground.

Rain started to fall as the round figure of Agnes entered the park. She trudged along the path, as she did every day to the duck pond. Her fat cheeks glowed from her tussle against the wind, and she looked rounder than ever in her brown mackintosh and blue wellingtons. She carried a bright bag, the only splash of colour on this dismal day.

As she walked along the path she almost stumbled over the limp form of Ernest. She was on her knees in an instant.

'Poor old man. I wonder who he is.' Gently she touched the cold face, and then, regardless of the weather, she took off her mackintosh and covered Ernest with it before hurrying as fast as her fat legs would take her to the telephone box by the park gates.

Some time later, after seeing the ambulance leave with Ernest inside, Agnes was feeding the ducks and wondering who the old man could be. He had no identification on him and nothing in his pockets but a door key and a handful of bird food. The shabby black bag was empty.

Back in Hope Street a familiar figure tripped gaily down the rain-soaked pavement. She hummed a merry little tune as the rain trickled down the gutters and gurgled down the drains. Freda, the home help, was doing her rounds. She knew almost all the residents and was welcomed into their homes.

Reaching the peeling green door, she tapped softly and tried to turn the handle, but the door was locked.

'Oh Ernest, you naughty boy. Surely you've never gone out in this weather. How many times have I told you that the pigeons won't starve if you miss just one day? I'll pop back later,' she said to herself, 'just as soon as I've finished the rest of the street.'

When Freda returned the door was still locked and this puzzled her. *I'll check at the office to see if he's away somewhere,* she thought, *but first I have to get Jane her dinner.*

Nine-year-old Jane skipped in from school. Taking off her wet clothes she went into the kitchen.

'What's for dinner, Mum?' she asked.

Freda smiled a welcome, 'Pie,' she answered, 'what better on a day like this?'

'Ooh super,' said Jane. 'I say, Mum, I've just seen Gran. She said she'd picked an old man up in the park today when she went to feed the ducks, and nobody knows who he is. They took him to Lane End Hospital. Poor old man - hey what's wrong, you look all in a tizz.'

'I think I know who he is,' her mother said, 'an old man did you say? And in the park? Oh Jane, I bet it's the Pigeon Man.'

'Who?' said Jane, 'the Pigeon Man. Who on Earth is that?'

'Well,' said Freda, 'it could be one of the poor old souls from Hope Street.'

'Ugh, that dump.' Jane wrinkled her nose in distaste. 'Why do you call him the Pigeon Man?'

'Well,' said Freda, reaching for the telephone directory, 'his real name is Ernest, but every morning, whatever the weather, he fills an old leather bag with food for the pigeons in the park. I've told him not to go when it's bad, but these old folks won't listen.'

'That's what you say about me,' laughed Jane, her eyes sparkling. 'Are you going to ring the hospital?'

'Mm, I think I'd better, for as far as I know he hasn't a living relative. Not in these parts anyway.'

Freda lifted the receiver and dialled the number.

'Lane End Hospital - can I help you?'

'I'm not sure,' replied Freda, 'I believe you admitted an old man today whose name you don't know.'

'That's right. Can you help?' said the voice.

'I hope so. I'm a home help and one of my old men wasn't at home today. He goes to the park every day to feed the pigeons. His name is Ernest Hepworth.'

'Ernest Hepworth,' repeated the voice, 'have you an address?'

'Hope Street. Number 34.'

'Thank you. Could you come along to the hospital to identify him?'

'Well - er - yes. He's not ...'

'No, no. He's confused, but will be all right. Just come when you can.'

Ernest was asleep when Freda called. 'Yes that's him,' she said. 'Tell him his home help called and will see him when he's back home.'

'I'll tell him, though he'll be here for some time yet.'

Ernest was sitting up in bed. He was beginning to feel better and as he did so he began to worry. *What will become of my feathered friends - and what will they think when I don't turn up? How long have I been here? I must get up and go to them.*

There didn't seem to be anyone about. Perhaps if he got up he could find his clothes. He pushed back the sheets and slid his legs over the side of the bed. Carefully he tried to stand up. *Crickey,* he felt a bit queer. His legs wouldn't hold him and he suddenly found himself in a heap on the floor.

The noise of his fall brought the young nurse dashing into his room.

'Now Ernest, what on Earth are you doing?' she gasped.

'I'm only going to feed the pigeons,' he said.

'They'll be all right. Come on, back to bed with you.'

'I want to go to the park,' he complained as she tucked him in-between the sheets.

'Not just yet I'm afraid, but cheer up. Here is a letter for you.'

'For me. Whoever would send letters to me? Read it to me love.'

The girl slit open the envelope, and took out a childish drawing of a pigeon signed 'Love from Jane'.

'Well I never,' he said, 'who is Jane?'

'Don't you know Ernest?' asked the nurse.

'Never heard of her,' he said, a puzzled frown appearing between his brows.

'That's one pigeon for you anyway,' laughed the nurse, 'so stay in bed now - there's a dear.'

Ernest looked at the picture and puzzled who Jane could be.

Next day another picture arrived of a man feeding the pigeons. This time, written in a childish hand were the words, 'Don't worry about the pigeons. Love from Jane'.

Who was she? Ernest just didn't know. Each day the pictures and the notes arrived, until one day, when the sun was shining, he was at last allowed home.

Ernest felt better and quite light-hearted, as he set off slightly later than had been his custom, to feed his beloved pigeons once more. Slowly he walked down Hope Street, and up past the shops until he turned in at the big iron gates. Crocuses were lifting their heads to the pale spring sunshine.

The pigeons saw him coming and soon the birds were everywhere, waiting while he threw the food to them from his shabby black bag. They remembered him, his feathered friends - oh it was good to be alive, he felt.

Ernest talked to them, calling them by name as he threw the last remaining scraps from his pockets. Then he turned to go. As he did so he saw, walking towards him, a little round woman carrying a red bag. A young girl was with her.

Suddenly the girl smiled and came running towards him.

'It's the Pigeon Man,' she cried, 'oh Mr Pigeon Man, are you better?'

Ernest looked at her in amazement. 'Are you Jane?' he asked.

'Yes. Did you get my pictures? Mummy told me you were ill. She's your home help, you know. Gran's been feeding your pigeons each day when she's come to feed the ducks. It was Gran who found you that day,' Jane said as Agnes waddled up.

'So it was you,' he said, 'and you've been looking after the birds for me.'

'No trouble,' said Agnes, 'I see they haven't forgotten you. Come with us and we'll feed the ducks together.' And so they did.

Freda knocked on the faded green door some months later and Ernest let her in with a smile.

'How's young Jane and that mother of yours?' he asked.

'They're fine, as well you know, seeing as how you see them every day, you old rogue,' she answered.

He laughed at that. 'I can't deny it,' he said, and then more seriously he added, 'we are great friends now.'

And so they were, the Pigeon Man, the Duck Lady and a dear little girl called Jane.

Arthur And The X-Ray Machine

Peter Asher

Had you been five years old and wanting to chop a big toe off your own foot then the latest equipment in Garden Shed Infirmary would have been ideal, for like all X-ray machines, if misused, it would have been dangerous.

It was thanks to Little Sheeps that this device towards health and healing was presently easing the workload for Staff and Poorly Boy alike - not because it was switched on and working, (because it didn't have a switch), but because it was stood there doing nothing. It was what Little Sheeps called 'The Mirror Model X-Ray Machine', and Nelly called 'The Plain Daft Smashed Mirror', because to be more accurate that's what it was.

It had started life as Dad's shaving mirror, becoming, when it was older, Poorly Boy's latest addition to The Onion Bench after he'd begged it when Mum bought Dad a new mirror which had a less flimsy support stand. Poorly Boy usually got whatever he pleaded for and Ben reluctantly, and against Sue's passionate counter pleadings, had seriously warned Poorly Boy against touching it once Ben had securely fixed it firmly to a strong wooden grooved plinth base containing the frame nearby the onions on Poorly Boy's Bench.

Only, Dad hadn't told Little Sheeps not to touch and as The Woolly One had plans for an X-ray machine which just happened to be based on a shaving mirror, all he needed to do was put a large crack in it with a piece of glass jaggedly removed some way or other, perfectly opened at the top about a child's toe width, tapering to a mere few centimetres at the bottom. Such a mirror length crack and gap could be obtained Little Sheeps felt, by standing Poorly Boy on tiptoes, raising Poorly Boy's arms and using Poorly Boy's hands to dislodge the mirror till it fell off The Onion Bench onto Garden Shed Infirmary floor, narrowly missing Poorly Boy's big toe.

That way, hopefully, the ideal crack for the job would be secured, though hardly the kind of safe security Dad had envisaged for his ex-shaving mirror's future.

To Little Sheeps' delight and - of course Poorly Boy's - the crack was perfect from top to bottom with only the plastic frame broken right through, a bit, they found after installing it back on The Bench on its new gliding, state-of-the-art onion base for quick and easy movement to anywhere in Garden Shed Infirmary or Poorly Boy's foot X-ray equipment might be needed to draw blood.

'You ain't using my machine properly, Poorly Boy.' Little Sheeps was irritated by Poorly Boy abusing his brain child. 'It's not really designed for flexing arm muscles in front of while our patients are kept waiting for important X-rays and no work's getting done.'

'Oh do shut up bleating, Little Sheeps.' Poorly Boy was irritated too, 'it was you who said I should do some training before lifting heavy weights and all I'm doing is making sure my arm muscles are standing up and ready for hard work!'

'It's also a great X-ray of the two halves of a Poorly Boy,' observed Nelly whilst being flexed in Poorly Boy's left X-ray plate, slit into two by a mirror with a dirty great crack up its middle with the missing piece of wedge-shaped glass lying on the floor waiting for Poorly Boy to cut himself - again - or else a poor team member or patient or Nelly! Nelly was not impressed by Little Sheeps' technological innovations in general, none of which she felt were boons to health. This one in particular had already claimed a small wound on one of the fingers smearing blood on her right now.

'Any case,' she went on, while Poorly Boy continued to flex and pump ever so small amounts of blood from his outstretched finger on and under her pink trunk, 'you don't even get to see inside of anything, only two halves and a dirty big crack.'

'Ye - but it's the 'crack' as you call it, which is the X-ray part itself,' pointed out the arm-tiring Poorly Boy.

'You're not supposed to see anything inside with this particular model, are you Little Sheeps, because it's more advanced than the simple sort of X-ray thingies you find in people hospitals.'

Nelly abruptly made Poorly Boy stop blood pumping. 'Then what use is it?' she glared into the mirror from above her blood-stained trunk.

Little Sheeps sighed exasperatedly. 'This is that powerful, you get to see right *through* things,' he said proudly. By way of clarification he continued in the manner all knowledgeable sheep lecture young flocks of pink lady elephants. "T'ain't no use seeing inside things with equipment now in use everywhere, cos with it being that plug into the wall type, all you get is very low power so the insides of objects spoil the view so you can't see right through them to the back of the equipment which is what is really wanted, because blood, guts, breath, bones, stitches and stuffing; all yucky stuff, gets in the way. This one. This one ...' he repeated for extra effect, 'is onion pong powered, and onion powered pongs are the pongiest, most powerful source of pong power unknown to man in the whole universal - but not …'

Poorly Boy was bowed low with raised arm to floor flourish, to salute the esteemed inventor who repeated for effect.

'But not, to Little Sheeps.'

As Little Sheeps finished his speech Poorly Boy stood up from his elaborate bow, his face deadpan serious as if defying everybody else's not to be. Nelly exasperated, sat the exhausted arm flexor in a heap with her on the woodchip floor.

Little Sheeps peered down at them from his elevated position of design genius on The Onion Bench next to his latest masterpiece. 'Are you ready to get with the morning's important job, Poorly Boy, or do we go on wasting time with ignoramusphants like Nelly till dinner?'

Nelly had lost too much blood to be bothered anymore. Poorly Boy stuck out his tongue as always when determined, sat Nelly lovingly gentle on the floor and stood, one aching arm holding the other helping it to flex. 'Right!' he exclaimed affirmatively, 'me 'n' Wheelbarrow/Ambulance is off to do what has to be done to do it properly.' With such wise words headaching in the ears of each soft toy and onion in Garden Shed Infirmary, Poorly Boy, all tiredness behind him and in jaw-jutting thrust of purpose doorwards, majestically swept out to the garden like a one wheeled red plastic pirate ship with an oddly dismembered face decoration on its four sides, followed by a stiff breeze of Captain Black Beard Poorly Boy at its two yellow tiller handles.

Garden Shed Infirmary fell silent in deep thought and ponder. Nelly looked into Little Sheeps' cunning eyes, Daddy Springy's wise ones, Crumble Bee's stupid ones and Baby Kenneth's curious ones as, on his nose end and dangerously close, Baby Kenneth examined the wickedly sharp triangular glass shard Little Sheeps had discarded while making X-rays possible. Not one of The Team spoke, though no doubt they deeply worried for the welfare of, if not their master, then their dearest human friend - for they would never have allowed Poorly Boy to be master over them. Would he, they no doubt wondered, survive his mission with his own health, only delicate at best, and little muscular power in his frail body? Most of all - would he persuade Mum, with the cunning Little Sheeps and Poorly Boy devised plan, behind the mission to let him keep the X-ray machine, though it could be dangerous in the wrong hands and paws? Nelly's bleakly doubting eyes, doubted it.

Joan was surprised to hear Poorly Boy's cheerful, 'Hello Joannie, can we come in and save you please? Mummy's with me and's given me permission!'

The day was warm and the window open, which gave a good view of Sue's puzzled and embarrassed shrug. Wheelbarrow/Ambulance stayed outside guarding the entrance as Joan, the old lady living next door, happily took Poorly Boy and Sue into the lounge where Poorly Boy - usually a small eater - unusually crumbled his way through three chocolate digestives. Joan loved having her young neighbours and she felt extra warmth towards them as it was the second time she'd been with Sue that morning. Today's company made her feel especially fond of them on account of Poorly Boy's obvious concern for her.

Joan and Sue watched fascinated while Poorly Boy caught crumbs planning escape from his plate with his finger end and gave his arms another flex to ensure the biscuits went to live in their muscles.

'Are you body building, Poorly Boy?' Joan chuckled. Sue coughed uneasily and spoke for her son, momentarily preoccupied crumb hunting.

'He says him and The Team have been waiting for the lorry to arrive but Daddy Springy says they must have missed it during their argument over Little Sheeps' X-ray machine.'

Joan, like most old people, was quicker on the uptake than those years younger and replied a couple of crumb hunt captives later that he must have somehow got confused while listening to her telling Sue about iron tablets.

'He must think I'm having a new path put down or something really heavy and the little treasure's come with his toy barrow and tiny muscles to lift and lay it for me! Oh what a beautiful, thoughtful child he is!'

Poorly Boy gave up the last crumb hunt when it ran into the carpet undergrowth beneath the table and escaped. Not to be beaten he chased after another biscuit with his hand inside the packet, rummaging for more tasty animal fat life at the bottom. 'No I ain't beautiful,' he spluttered indignantly, disdain dribbling full-mouthed and chocolate chin to T-shirt. 'I didn't want you carrying iron tablets once the big men had delivered the massive box that's all. They're really heavy they are and anyway me and The Team aren't sure the doctor's right when he tells you you're short of metal. You're very old to be swallowing that much iron. One thing it could rust wiv the water you drink and another it means your Arthur's going to get worse too with the extra weight he's got to lift if you fall over.'

New Fiction - Hickory Dickory

Joan quickly realised her long dead husband hadn't been called Arthur and Poorly Boy must mean her arthritis.

But Poorly Boy had no time to lose and had a point to prove. 'Come on then, let's go to Little Sheeps' machine before Mum throws it out. Stand clear Joannie and Mum while I carry the big box of iron tablets out to Wheelbarrow/Ambulance and we go to Garden Shed Infirmary. Where are you keeping such a huge package, it's not sticking out from anywhere - have you left it round the side of the house cos it's too big to get through the door? Don't worry, I can split things into smaller chunks with my plastic saw. Lorry drivers are like my dad and in a hurry to do everything in a hurry to hurry up and spoil everything they do, Mum says, so they'll have cleared off and left you to it, like Dad does Mum.'

Joan noticed, then withdrew her glance quickly, how Sue flushed red.

Poorly Boy was surprised and disappointed at the smallness of the box of tablets when Joan pointed it out on the table at which Poorly Boy was seated with them so near his plate he'd been playing with the box while eating. The scowl lasted long enough to brood he'd be unable to show how strong he was to the two grown-ups and The Team, before blossoming into the realisation his slight concern over his poorly heart's weight lifting abilities wouldn't be tested after all, so at least he ought to still be alive when they reached Garden Shed Infirmary to show off Little Sheeps' technological brain lamb.

He was still insistent he carry the tablets outside to place in Wheelbarrow/Ambulance, Mum protesting and warning him not to fall with or damage them in any way, while he protested back that if she'd really been a good, caring mother, she'd be more worried about his poorly heart falling over than the silly box's heart getting squished. Joan meanwhile strolled behind this carnival, an amused smile on her lined but well entertained face.

At the ever half open door to Garden Shed Infirmary, Poorly Boy stopped arguing and turned to face Mum, his arms raised, hands opened as if stilling chattering hordes before an important speech. 'Now Mum - don't go on at Little Sheeps when you see his invention, cos you won't like it, you'll say it's dangerous and that it's got to go. Just be careful that when you yell at him you do it softly as he's sheepish and easily hurt, his ears are bad and his legs easily break.' He stopped and pushed his right palm against the air, testing to make sure it was still holding Mum fast behind it. 'I dun't mind you chucking it out, but only if you promise before you go in to let Little Sheeps do what he has to do with it before it goes out.'

Sue opened her mouth to yell at Poorly Boy like any mum would in this situation - but the air rushed in to prevent her, or rather Joan's light and spry unconcerned, 'Of course we don't mind Little Sheeps using his dangerous machine, do we Sue, we trust him and you, sweetheart, and know you're only doing the best for my tablets and me. Promise there's no electricals involved though, won't you?' she added as the sole cautionary note.

Poorly Boy withdrew his arms and rushed inside accompanied by the air.

Naturally, Sue spluttered when she saw Ben's ex-shaving mirror and in the same splutter learnt from Joan's pointed finger towards Poorly Boy and The Onion Bench that this indeed was the home of the unique and sensitive machine. Joan's eyes were as big as the plaques on her living room walls, and it seemed Mum looked in need of a chair to either sit on or brain her only child with.

'Now - watch,' announced the only child. 'Joan,' Poorly Boy looked up at the old lady, his eyes bigger and more charming than any wall plate or sun smiling an April shower away, 'may I please pass an iron pill to Little Sheeps for X-ray?'

Joan nodded an eager affirmative and as Poorly Boy broke the seal and carried regally a tiny white capsule outstretched towards Little Sheeps (the palm of one hand with pill being supported underneath by the other as if it weighed a steel town full of foundries) he explained what was going on. 'You see, as Little Sheeps tells me to hold the iron up in front of the machine's screens, or broke mirror for those who don't understand such things as this - there is nothing to be seen and the tablet becomes invisible in the middle of the bit where the glass is missing.'

Poorly Boy's brows were drawn low and met in the middle giving him a severe look. 'That isn't because the tablet is too small to be shown back because there's a whacking great piece of glass missing out of the middle - so don't say it is!'

None did.

'It is because there is very little iron in these tablets the doctor has given Joannie to take.' He turned to the women; the professor towards his class, 'This means with the machine set to X-ray for any Iron present in the tablet's tummy and finding not even enough to show a little picture of - then if Joannie was to swallow the whole lot at once, her Arthur wouldn't have to worry none about her ever moving again because she was too heavy. He wouldn't need a crane or wheels fitted to her or margarine the floor to slide her on neither, isn't Little Sheeps clever?'

Even one as young as Baby Kenneth looked up at Poorly Boy as if his explanation of a difficult procedure was good enough for baby rabbits and thus fully grown women. Poorly Boy frowned even deeper in the silence following Little Sheeps' demonstration. Surely Baby Kenneth had been on his nose when he'd last seen him and nobody there had noticed or moved him. That piece of glass X-ray machine Little Sheeps had thrown on the floor unwanted; that piece looking very sharp and nasty - wasn't it closer to Baby Kenneth's nose when he last saw it, not close by The Onion Bench glinting at him on top of the full rubbish bin? Must have been the breeze or Arthur that warned Baby Kenneth to stay away from sharp edges and blew or put the glinty bit out of harm's way.

'Come on!' said Sue, breaking Poorly Boy's train of thought. It was then he also caught sight of what appeared to be a blue plastic handle propped just the other side of the bin by The Onion Bench. 'Now we know it's safe for Joan to take such small amounts of iron, we'd better go and have a cup of tea. It's about time for her dose.' There was a curious sort of laughter tone in Sue's voice which made Poorly Boy look at her suspiciously. She smiled; a perfectly innocent gleaming at him.

'Oh there it is - pass me my blue dustpan propped by The Onion Bench will you Poorly Boy. Arthur must have left it behind after we'd heard a crash of glass earlier this morning and he'd peered round Garden Shed Infirmary door and saw you all working hard. He came and told me everything was alright though, no harm done and it was only Little Sheeps constructing a strange machine. May I try it before I get rid of it in the bin Poorly Boy? See if it can see right through me like I can you?' But Poorly Boy didn't really hear - he was too angry with Arthur. What a sneak. No wonder he kept out the way and you never caught sight of him creeping round causing trouble and spoiling plans.

Little Davey And The Magical Fruit

Stuart Brierley

A long time ago there was a boy called Davey and because he was very small everyone called him Little Davey, soon even his mum and dad called him Little Davey.

Little Davey was five years old and had no friends at all. He played on his own, he ate on his own and, because he had no brothers or sisters, he even slept on his own. He had lots of toys but did not have anyone to play with and so he got very upset.

One day Little Davey stopped playing with his toys and began to cry.

Little Davey cried every day but no one ever saw him. Even his mum and dad never saw that their Little Davey spent every day alone in his room, crying. Little Davey felt like no one cared about him and so that night he went out on his own, even though it was very dark outside.

As Little Davey was only five years old he did not know what to do or where to go so he walked and walked and walked, until his little legs got so tired that they stopped and he stood still.

Little Davey looked around, it was then that he saw the fruit store. The fruit store was the only store that sold every kind of fruit in the world. Little Davey saw the fruit through the store window and this made him feel very hungry. He looked for a way to get inside the fruit store but could not find a way in and so he began to cry again.

Little Davey was still crying when he saw a black and white cat go round to the back of the fruit store. Davey knew the black and white cat's name was Curly and he belonged to Mr Green who worked in the fruit store. Little Davey went with the black and white cat through the cat flap in the back door of the store and once he was inside he began to look for fruit to eat.

He ate an apple, a pear, a banana and even a peach. When he was full up, he turned to face the fruit that he had not eaten and said, 'Thank you for making me so full up! I am not hungry anymore.' Little Davey then turned away from the fruit and began to walk slowly as he made his way to the cat flap on the back door of the fruit store.

As Little Davey got to the cat flap he began to hear the words 'you're welcome' being said, over and over again. He turned back to look at the fruit in the fruit store, he was looking to see who had said 'you're welcome'.

By this time, all was quiet again so Little Davey turned back to face the cat flap and said out loud, 'Well, there is no one in here.' He then very quickly turned back to face the fruit once more and …

He was amazed to see that the fruits were all talking and all the fruits had faces, arms and legs. You see, smart Little Davey had known that once he turned his back again he would hear 'you're welcome' so he played a trick and turned back as quick as he could to catch who it was that was talking.

Little Davey said to himself, 'It's magic,' as he stood there looking at the fruits, his mouth and eyes wide open, he could not believe what he was seeing. It was then that the fruits began to tell Little Davey who they were, one by one they began to say their names.

'Hi, my name is Olly Orange.'

'Hi, I'm Annie Apple.'

'Hello, my name's Percy Pear.'

'I'm Bertie Banana, howdie!' and on the fruits went until they had all said their names.

After they had finished, they all said at once, 'Nice to meet you.'

'Hi, my name is Davey,' replied the boy, in awe, 'but people call me Little Davey because I'm so small.'

The fruits told him that they were smaller than he so they would call him Davey, as this was his real name after all. Little Davey felt so big for the first time ever and was so happy that he now had many new friends.

Davey told his new friends that it was time to go home for the night and that he would come to see them all every night, and that is just what he did. Davey had many adventures as he grew older with the many fruits, and to this day Davey and the fruits are still good friends.

A Winter's Tale

Ariana Luisa Chiarelli

It was a cold winter's morning and tiny snowflakes were falling from the clear blue sky. The snow lay thick on the ground and the leaves fallen from the trees were all gathered underneath.

The trees were swaying as if they were shivering. Under a tree stump was a rabbit burrow, and there lived a family of four rabbits. The parents had two little rabbits called Bella and Baby.

Bella was known for her bossiness, showing off and telling everyone what to do. She had long floppy ears and a black twitchy nose. She had a white body with black patches on, and a black circle patch around her right eye.

Baby was known for her shyness, generosity and quietness. She had long floppy ears and a brown twitchy nose, she also had a white body but with a brown patch on her back in the shape of a butterfly, and a brown circle patch around her right eye.

On a Monday morning, Bella and Baby were scurrying around in the snow, they were building snowmen and jumping over each other's backs. 'Shall we go home now and have lunch? I'm starving!' said Bella, and bounced up to Baby and led her back to the burrow.

Once they got there, they both scurried to their parents' bedroom, but they were not in there, all they saw was the bed and a pile of leaves, that had never been there before. It was rustling and something hopped out, that gave Bella and Baby a fright.

'*Argh!* Run! Run! Run as fast as you can!' Bella cried out. Baby ran as fast as her little legs could carry her, they ran so fast they did not realise where they were going. With a crash, bang and a wallop, they both fell in a heap on the leafy floor, trees surrounded them, and not a single bird was singing.

'How are we going to get home?' whimpered Baby, tears dripping from her furry cheeks.

Bella understood that Baby was scared, but for the first time in her life, she felt scared as well. 'We will ask someone on the way,' Bella replied.

'But what way?' Baby asked.

'Whatever way we find,' Bella said gloomily.

They both rose to their feet and started to jump straight ahead of them.

The hours turned to days as Bella and Baby hopped on the trail, but luckily there were fallen berries and leaves on the floor so they stopped to have a nibble for a few minutes.

One day, they were walking across a familiar snowy meadow when Baby suddenly heard a rustle. 'W … w … w … what's that n … n … n … noise?' she trembled, making Bella spring into action.

'Quick! Run! Run to that familiar tree stump over there! Run!' Bella shouted, and she and Baby raced over to the tree stump.

As they ran, a fox jumped out behind them and started to try and pounce on them.

Bella and Baby finally got to it and dived in. Baby locked the door and sighed with relief. They suddenly both fell quiet and looked around the room. It was their own living room! They had made it!

'Home!' squealed Bella and Baby. Suddenly, their beady eyes fell upon moving creatures in the room, it was their mum and dad! They both hurried to them and gave them a huge hug.

'Where were you both? Me and your dad have been looking all over for you two!' Mum cried out.

Then Bella and Baby told them about their adventures.

'That's weird, I was under a pile of leaves, I looked up and saw you two, but you screamed and ran off before I could say anything,' said Mum.

'Sorry! We thought you were a fox!' chanted Bella and Baby together.

After that, they all tucked into a stew Mum had made. Of course, it was a carrot stew, not a *rabbit stew*. They wouldn't dream of that!

Golden Mermaid

Jenifer Ellen Austin

A long time ago, there lived a very beautiful little girl. She lived with her family and other villagers near a forest.

The little girl looked different from other boys and girls so, sadly, her family didn't love her anymore. They called her names, they kept hitting her, they always made her cry. They treated her very badly.

Her family didn't want her living with them anymore. They had heard about beasts that roamed the forest and ate up boys or girls that had been lost or abandoned.

One day her nasty, evil family took the little girl out into the forest to leave her there all by herself for those big, nasty, ugly beasts to eat her up.

The little girl was very frightened being alone inside the dark forest. She could hear the beasts roaring in the distance as they were chasing lost children. She could hear the piercing screams of frightened children as they were shouting as loud as they could for help, and running as fast as they could as the beasts were chasing them, until there were no screams any more. The little girl knew these beasts were feasting on all the children they had killed.

The little girl didn't know why her family were so nasty to her, or why they had left her there all alone in the dark forest with all the child-eating beasts hoping she would be the beasts' next meal.

The little girl didn't know why her family had left her there all on her own in the forest. She didn't know why they had treated her so badly at home. Her family were cruel because when she was born she had no legs or feet.

The little girl's family were very selfish. They believed they couldn't love the little girl because of the way she looked. It repulsed her family just to look at her; to them she was rubbish waiting to be disposed of at their convenience. They didn't have the wisdom to know how very beautiful, loving and special the little girl was.

The little girl became more and more hungry; colder and colder,; more and more frightened. She became very tired as she tried to hide herself away from the forest beasts that were searching for her.

She had now been left in the forest for many hours and had given up all hope of anyone ever finding her. She had given up all hope of anyone being kind enough to help take care of her.

She started to cry but was afraid that if she made a noise the beasts of the forest would hear her. She kept on crying and crying, silently to herself. Eventually she became too tired, cold and hungry to go on. She collapsed on the forest floor with exhaustion, crying herself to sleep.

When the girl woke up, she thought she must be in Heaven. 'If I am not in Heaven, I must be dreaming,' she said to herself. She was not in Heaven and she was not dreaming, there were birds flying above and all around her.

The birds knew there were beasts in the forest. The beasts had eaten some of their friends. When the birds heard the little girl silently crying before she fell asleep, they knew she was in danger. They flew as fast as they could into the dark forest to find her.

Soon they became solid friends. The birds stayed with the little girl wherever she went, protecting her, loving her and never leaving her alone again. They made her some clothes out of their feathers to keep her warm. They gathered nuts and berries off trees outside the forest then flew down and dropped the food onto her hand.

She could only move by putting her hands in front of her and lifting her body up and swinging herself over to rest. Repeating this same sequence over and over again made all the skin come off her hands.

The little girl's face became scarred with all the crying she had done in the past. Her heart became scarred with all the heartache that it had suffered. Soon her heart was too scarred to be mended. She became very ill. It made her very tired and she fell into a deep sleep. The little girl's bird friends flew around her, keeping watch over her and making sure no harm came to her as she slept and slept and slept.

When the little girl was still in her deep sleep her bird friends wanted her to know just how much they loved her. Hoping she would hear them singing enough to wake her up from her deep sleep.

She did hear the birds singing. One day the little girl did begin to slowly wake up and as she did so she heard a funny, strange voice-like noise. It wasn't the birds singing, it wasn't the forest beasts. She managed to find some courage and be brave enough to have a look at where the strange voices were coming from. Her eyes were met with the sight of little people, no more than an inch high. They were transparent with lovely rainbow auras twinkling beautifully.

Unknown to the little girl these rainbow people were watching over her as she lay in a deep sleep and had made her a pair of golden hands.

The little girl soon discovered how magical the little people were. They twinkled like diamonds, rubies, sapphires, emeralds, crystal, silver and gold. They were magical, loving, beautiful people with many loving ways. She called these little people her magic rainbow friends.

Her magic rainbow friends could see how badly scarred her face had been left from all the crying she had done. They loved her very much and made her a new, very beautiful face that had a golden glow that shone so brightly it dazzled anyone or any beasts that came to do her harm.

The magic rainbow friends had been so busy making the girl her new golden hands and face that they hadn't seen she had no legs or feet. It made her magic rainbow friends become very sad.

All the excitement of having her golden hands and face made the little girl become tired and she fell into another deep sleep. Whilst she lay sleeping, her friends wanted to make her a pair of magic golden mermaid's flippers to match her hands and face.

After many seasons had passed, the little girl's rainbow friends had seen the little girl starting to wake up. They all waited with much excitement to show her what they had made her and how happy she was going to be.

When the little girl eventually woke up she wondered why all her magic rainbow friends and bird friends were all around her, looking at her, smiling with much happiness as she looked down to see her golden flipper. She looked very beautiful, happy and felt loved very much by all her friends in the forest.

The magic rainbow friends asked the little girl to go and live with them in their secret magic home in the forest. She happily lived with them for a very long time.

When the little girl was mistreated badly by her family it left her heart scarred. The scarring had started to make the little girl become ill. Her friends were very worried and they didn't know what to do. One day she stopped breathing, her heart stopped beating, she lay dead in front of them and there was nothing any of them could do to help her.

The little girl's friends could not stop crying. They cried so much that their tears flowed to one end of the forest, making a magical sea. In this sea there were dolphins, coral reefs, lots of hidden caves, many treasures and much beauty all around.

The sea became bigger and bigger with the little girl's friends' tears. Soon the sea became an ocean, as her friends would make the long journey out of the forest to sit beside the sea crying over the little girl's death.

It was a long, hard journey for the rainbow friends to go to the sea to mourn their friend's death. Often they would fall asleep on the sea bank, others would go back to the forest still crying.

One of the little girl's magic rainbow friends was upset that they had so much magic but could do nothing to save their much-loved friend from death; he just knew he had to find some way of bringing her back to life. He thought and thought and thought all night and all day long until he had an idea of how he could make the magic work for their friend.

I know, I can give the little girl my heart, he thought. He quickly woke up the others to tell them his idea. They all ran back as fast as they could into the forest to their secret home and told the others to start working on giving the little girl his heart.

Three of the rainbow friends gave the little girl some magic healing before they could place their friend's heart inside her. As they were doing this, one of the friends began to cry. He realised that the heart they were going to place inside her was too small. Soon every one of them was crying again, their tears were flowing into the sea.

The sea became sad for all the magic rainbow friends and started to cry. It could not stop crying. Soon the Sea God felt and heard all the tears being cried. He asked, 'Why is there all this sadness in the sea?'

One of the magic rainbow friends told the Sea God of the plight of their little friend. The Sea God became very sad with what he was told and he started to cry.

The Sea God wanted to help the little girl and her rainbow friends, he grabbed a magic wand as he came out of the sea and took it with him into the forest to where the little girl was lying to wave the wand over her lifeless body. It did not work. The little girl lay lifeless.

The Sea God had another idea, make the girl a magic heart! Everyone went to work, day and night, until a magic heart had been made. The magic heart was placed inside the little girl; the Sea God waved his magic wand over the little girl. Nothing happened. He did it again, nothing happened. By now everyone began to believe they were never going to see their friend again.

The little girl's bird friends started to sing loudly as they flew around her lifeless body. The Sea God thought he had seen a slight breathing motion from the girl. Quickly he waved his magic wand over the girl and told her bird friends to sing as loud and as lovingly as they could. It was working, the little girl was being brought back to life again.

There was one huge party to celebrate the little girl being alive. When the party was over, all her friends followed the Sea God, carrying the little girl to the edge of the forest and into the sea. All her magic rainbow friends and bird friends waved goodbye as she gently disappeared into the sea, where she was to live until she made a full recovery with the Sea God's friends where they loved and cared for her very much, naming her Golden Mermaid.

Golden Mermaid has often been seen protecting and talking to lost, lonely, frightened, unloved children on the edge of the forest, near the sea.

When I am lost, lonely, frightened, crying and always unloved. I go to a place where I can find my own sea. As I bow my head, all my tears fall out from me into the sea. I raise my head and glance across the sea's horizon. On it, I see a dazzling golden light shining back to me.

Jo Jo

David R Morgan

'Is Jo Jo starlight now?' asked Rebecca, the day after her grandma died.

'Yes,' said Dad, 'I think she is.'

Years before, as a little girl, Jo Jo had made friends with the night-time stars. Like living fireworks, she understood their stories and so, as she grew, no whispering shadows could ever sneak through.

Jo Jo told the stars' stories to her son and then to her little granddaughter, Rebecca. 'Look, there's Ursa Major, there's Ursa Minor and there's Orion's Belt smiling at us,' said Jo Jo dancing, and as she danced it seemed as though she was surrounded by sparkling starlight. Rebecca's nights were magic.

And then the magic died.

'If Grandma is starlight now,' Rebecca said, 'can I see her?'

'Perhaps,' said Dad, 'if you need to enough.'

Rebecca gazed through her bedroom window. 'Twinkle, twinkle, Grandma Starlight, show me where you are tonight.' But the magic was hidden from her.

The following night Rebecca repeated her rhyme; still nothing ... but something *was* coming.

The whispering shadow came as Rebecca lay in bed. It was a strange little dog whispering in her ear; naughty, playing with her toys, doing silly things. Rebecca hardly slept at all.

The next night more whispering shadows came. They were big bugs; very naughty; whispering all the time, bouncing off walls, webbing ceilings, scuttling about, never staying still. Rebecca got very fed up.

On the third night, whispering shadows flooded Rebecca's bedroom. They were large fish swimming in the air, with nasty big mouths blowing bubbles that burst noisily, *pop, pop, pop.* The crazy fish circled, looped, spun, darted and swirled. They surrounded Rebecca and she felt like she was trapped in some mad fish tank. She didn't know what to do. She pleaded, 'Grandma Starlight, please, please show me your magic tonight!'

Suddenly, starlight sparkled into her bedroom, zigzagging it with magic.

Each whispering shadow fell silent. Each whispering shadow became luminous as the starlight touched it. Each whispering shadow dropped to the floor flapping, gasping and then popping like a burst bubble and disappearing.

'Thank you for coming back to me Jo Jo,' said Rebecca. She got into bed and fell soundly, peacefully asleep ...

In the night-time sky, Grandma Starlight smiled.

Loafer The Beagle

Gerard Allardyce

Somewhere in the countryside of the south ...

In the town of Tochester, deep in the heart of the south country, a fox hunt was about to take place. As usual for such an event, the townsfolk had come out in their droves to support the spectacle. The local hunt had created jobs for the locals and they cheered those taking part.

Our story, children, takes part in the middle of the nineteenth century at a time when cockfighting and bare-fist boxing were also popular.

Ralph Smith was outside Acres the Bakers watching the horsemen assemble in their brightly-coloured red tunics and top hats.

'That's Sir Mark Hubbard. He is the Master of the Hunt.'

'What does that mean, Daddy?'

'Didn't they tell you that at school?' he said to his ten-year-old son. 'The Master of the Hunt is in charge of the sport. He blows his horn to mark the start of the fox hunt and for the horses and their riders to gallop and the beagles to run and smell out the foxes and destroy them and then, when the dog has caught the fox, to end it all by blowing the horn heartily again.'

'Does that mean the fox hunt is over, Daddy?'

'What did I say, Robert? Of course when the Master of the Hunt blows his horn the hunt is over. You know, Robert, when I tell you something you must listen. They are about to pass through the town. I've always thought, Robert, it is a fine occasion and that is something your children's children will also agree.'

The beagles were in front of the pack, as usual, and the horsemen in hot pursuit in the fields. There was a yelping from the dogs. The Master of the Hunt blew his horn and they were off, with the horses snorting and neighing in the general melee. Soon the hunt was far out of the town of Tochester, crossing the ancient stone bridge that crossed the river, teeming as it always had been with trout chattering happily.

Within minutes, the sunshine and blue sky had given way to blinding rain and a fierce wind. The beagles and horses were being covered with mud and the dogs were slipping and sliding all over the place. Muddy fields were indeed slowing the hunt and the beagles and horses were soon panting and labouring as the weather worsened.

Now, girls and boys, our attention is on an old beagle by the name of Loafer. Far from being a loafer he was amongst the fastest hounds in the pack, but that was a long time ago. At the time of writing, Loafer was fifteen years old and had never been bred. For the last year, the Master of the Hunt in particular, had whipped him and scolded him for being a slow coach and straggling behind all the other beagles. Loafer felt he was nearing the end of his days and his arthritic bones gave him great pain, poor Loafer. Once upon a time he was the best and fastest beagle in the Tochester hunt. Now all he could think about was death, and the approach of it filled him with dread. Once more he had straggled far behind the pack where the nasty beagle, Snaker, had savaged and torn a fox to pieces. That is the sort of thing Loafer never did in his prime. He believed in a quick mercy kill and a bite delivered behind the fox's neck. Now as he struggled behind the pack he knew that this time he would be put down, for he was, as a human would say, 'surplus to requirement'.

'Get on wi' thee,' the Master of the Hunt shouted as he brought his whip down on the poor back of Loafer. He gave a whimper of pain. 'You'll be put down if you don't buck your ideas up, Loafer.'

Then Loafer barked angrily and with all the strength he could muster, he jumped all of three feet to be level with the horse and rider and bit the Master of the Hunt's leg. Then Loafer, children, summoning all his strength, ran away from the horsemen and the pack.

'After him,' the Master of the Hunt cried, but try as they might, horses and beagles could not catch up with Loafer, who ran with no fear, barking as he went to keep up his morale in the blinding rain and tempest. At last, the pack and the horsemen gave up following him and Loafer felt the taste of freedom for the first time since he had been born fifteen years or so before.

At last he found himself in a woodland where, children, this thirsty old beagle found a stream and drank much water from it. He trundled up the bank of the stream wondering what on Earth to do next and how to avoid the terrible death that awaited him in the town, when he came across a hare sitting on a large tree stump. There was something strange and mildly refreshing about this hare. He wore a top hat, black waistcoat, and carried an umbrella.

'Hello, Loafer,' the hare said in a high-pitched voice.

'How do you know my name? And for that matter, what's yours?' and Loafer gave a growl just like in the old days.

'Glad you can still growl in that manner, Loafer. You will need to and that is not meant in a bad sense, Loafer. By the way, all the woodland creatures know you in the south country and abroad as a good dog who is a friend of all the little animals, in particular the foxes. They remember, those affectionate foxes, how you let them run away one by one when you caught them in the good old days, and by the way, my name is Lardus the hare.'

'Lardus is a funny name for a hare,' said Loafer, quaintly amused by this clever creature.

'I am descended from a hare called Dradis that belonged to Merlin the wizard in the good old days of King Arthur's Knights and the Round Table. I can help you and already I have done so. The horsemen will never find you, neither will their pack of beagles. I have cast magic spells throughout the south country as of two moons ago and you cannot be found and nothing but good things will come to you. Are you hungry? I know you were thirsty.'

'I am so, so very hungry, Lardis,' Loafer replied and he barked quietly as beagles do.

'Fancy a Big Mac?'

'Yes please.'

And with that Lardis waved his umbrella and a double burger in a bun with ketchup emerged on the tree stump and Loafer ate it with pleasure in his very being.

'Fancy cheese and pickle?'

'Yes please, Lardis.'

Once more, Loafer ate with carefree abandon on the tree stump where the sandwiches appeared.

'Fancy ham and tomato with salad garnish?'

'Yes please,' Loafer replied once again and perhaps he enjoyed those two rounds more than anything else.

'What have I done to deserve this treatment?' asked Loafer.

'Because you have been kind to all the creatures of the forest, you are, Loafer, going to get your just reward … a woman, Loafer, a lady dog, just three and a half years old and you will sire at least eight offspring of either sex that will resemble you and her … the distinctive brown patches on a white background. You will live in a fox lair big enough for the king you are. We will be with this lovely lady in a minute or two.'

'What's her name, Lardis?'

'Cassie. Can you hear her youthful bark ahead of us in the forest?'

'I certainly can, Lardis.'

'Goodbye, Loafer,' and the magical hare was gone.

'Hello, Cassie,' Loafer grumbled in a doggy language.

'Hello, Loafer ... I heard all about you and deserted my hunt in the north country to be with you.'

'That's a long way, Cassie ...'

'Nothing is too far for such a wonderful and great champion to us all.'

And with that, children, Loafer and Cassie lived happily ever after.

The Wallabies In The Tree House

Barbara Russell

Once upon a time a family of five wallabies lived on an enormous farm in the middle of the forest. On the farm there were cows, horses, sheep, goats, pigs, rabbits, hens and a large lake with several ducks. The farm was picturesque and all the animals were well cared for.

The wallabies were a very close family, they always looked out for each other. Bess and Berty who were the mother and father, and their three babies, Billy, Barney and Blossom. The two boys took great care of their sister; wherever they went they made sure she was not far behind.

Every morning the owner of the farm, whose name was Jack, would come round and give all the animals their breakfast. After breakfast, the rest of the day would be spent running about, and having fun. Quite often people would visit the farm and children would bring treats for the animals. It was a happy place to be. Bess and Berty had lived on the farm for many years, and they loved each other very much.

At night-time the family would gather, and snuggle up together under a bush to keep each other warm. If it was a very cold night, they would go into the shelter. As long as they were all together, they were content.

Billy, Barney and Blossom were getting big now. They would run about all day and tire themselves out. Sometimes they would have little fights but it was all in fun and they would never do each other any harm.

One cold winter night, they all settled down for bed as usual. After a very hectic day, they soon fell asleep. Then, disaster struck: a very loud howling could be heard and it was coming form the forest but because they were so tired, they were still in a deep sleep. Apart from Bess; she was disturbed by the noise. She did her best to ignore it, but it got louder and louder. Instead of waking Berty, she decided to go outside to see what was causing the disturbance. As she did, she saw a huge animal but because it was so dark she could not tell what it was. From that point on, everything happened so quickly. The bear-like animal struck its teeth into her neck, and ran off into the forest with her. She was terrified: she tried to raise the alarm by making an awful noise, but her cries were not heard.

Berty was the first to wake in the morning; he was puzzled when he saw Bess was not beside him. He woke the family and they all went outside to look for their mother. After a while, panic set in, and Berty realised something had must have happened to her. They spent the day searching only to get more disheartened.

As night-time approached, Berty decided it was not safe to stay where they were so he gathered them up, and took them into the forest.

They had been on the move for a while and Blossom was very tired. *Not much further,* Berty thought, *and we will be at the tree house, where we will stay for a while.* He knew they would be safe there. He had found it some time ago, when he had been exploring the forest with Bess. It was their favourite place. Finally the tree house came into sight. Five more minutes and their journey would be over. Billy and Barney were crying for their mother, and Berty was trying to comfort them.

Now they were safe. The only problem was the tree house had no door, but he knew he would be able to sort that out later. All they wanted now was to go to sleep, after a long, hard and very sad day.

The next day, Berty's priority was to find a large piece of wood that they could use for a door. Eventually, he found one, and he made it safe. Things were different now; they all had to go out and find their own food, they no longer had Jack to provide for them.

Berty was missing Bess very much, if only he knew what had happened to her. He tried to put on a brave face in front of his family but, deep down, his heart was broken. The days were long, and the nights even longer. Since Bess had gone, he was finding it hard to sleep. Most of the night he would stand at the door almost like he was on guard.

A few nights passed by and then something very strange happened. Billy, Barney and Blossom were asleep, Berty could not settle because he kept hearing a strange, eerie noise. He opened the door and, in the distance, he could see what he thought was Bess. It was a white object, sat motionless, looking at the tree house. He called her name out loud and to his amazement the object disappeared into thin air. *Was it Bess?* he thought, *or was it a ghost?* He was mystified, and at the same time he was frightened. He decided he was imagining all this because he was so tired. Finally he got off to sleep, but his first thought in the morning, was what he saw in the night.

For the next four nights the same white object that resembled Bess appeared, opposite the tree house. If he did not move or make a noise it would stay there, but as soon as he muttered a sound, it disappeared. Bert was convinced now, that Bess was dead and that it was her ghost. *Perhaps she has come back to guard us*, he thought.

He could not face another night in the tree house: he decided to return to the farm. At least they would all get regular food and he might even sleep better. So they all set off back to familiar territory. When they arrived they were greeted by Jack who was beside himself with worry. He realised why they had left but he was not sure what had made them return. Then he said excitedly, 'Come with me,' and he lead the wallabies into a large pen. They could not believe their eyes: Bess lay there, all snug and comfortable. The young ones shrieked with happiness. Their mother was back. She had been badly attacked and left in the forest for dead. A hiker had found her and brought her back to the farm. She had been operated on by the vet, and had spent the last few days recovering. Berty cried with happiness. He was forever thankful to the ghost for making him come back to the farm.

Sidney The Brain Cell And The Amazing Drop

Linda Knight

Sidney woke up with a jolt and found himself dropping down inside a big dark hole. Suddenly he was surrounded by a blue light that cradled his fall and as he gently floated in the air, Something from Somewhere said, 'Hello Sidney.'

Sidney recognised the voice of his friend.

'Where did you come from Something?' he said.

'Oh nowhere in particular,' said Something.

The light whisked them away sideways at great speed and stopped just as quickly, dumping them with a bump into a pile of red sand. Sidney landed face down and he coughed and spluttered. Getting up, he looked around wondering where this very cold place was. Mountains of red sand surrounded him, and up above the sky was green. *How peculiar*, he thought.

Something from Somewhere landed a few feet away. Rubbing his head and feeling a bit giddy, he said, 'The world's going round and round.'

Sidney pointed to a large sand dune just ahead. 'Let's climb up there and find out where we are.'

They were tired, cold and hungry and as they reached the top, Sidney looked across at more red sand. 'Oh, Something, what are we going to do?'

The sand that Sidney and Something were standing on suddenly shifted, and they slid down the steep slope, straight into another deep hole.

'Help, help, where are we going, oh no!'

They fell into the darkness.

Once again they landed with a bump, but this time it was very different. They were met by a group of creatures very curious at seeing these two new arrivals.

'Sidney, they can see me,' said Something, who used to be Nothing from Nowhere, and was usually invisible.

'Perhaps they have special eyes to be able to see things that others can't,' said Sidney.

The little creatures were grey in colour with two large feelers on their heads, two enormous yellow eyes and six legs. They wore eight solid bands of armour plating around their bodies. They seemed friendly enough and many more creatures came out to have a look, as they led Sidney and Something over to some caves. The cave walls were covered in paintings about the little grey creatures, and Sidney went to have a closer look at them. He couldn't believe his eyes when he saw a picture of himself and Something riding on a large white moth, leading the little grey creatures into some kind of battle. 'Looks like we are here to help out,' said Sidney to Something.

They were given some odd looking food that tasted very nice and given a drink from the liquid that ran down the walls, and then, feeling very tired, they fell asleep.

They woke up to a tremendous noise going on. The little grey creatures were rushing out of the caves and into a hole that led upwards.

'Come on, Something, let's join them and see what's happening.'

'Alright, Sidney, here we go, up and away!'

In the hole there were other tunnels leading off and Sidney could see small bats being harnessed and ridden forward through the tunnels, and up towards the light. Some of the little creatures urged Sidney and Something into a larger tunnel where a very big furry moth waited. Attached to its head was a gold bridle, and strapped to its body a double gold saddle. They beckoned Sidney and Something to get on, and the huge moth crawled up into the light, flying off to join the bats in the green sky.

They flew off in a long line towards the north. Later, in the distance Sidney could see a large city that glowed dark red. Above it, a large black cloud formed and moved very rapidly in their direction.

The little grey creatures lined up their flying groups with Sidney out in front on the enormous white furry moth.

'Something, I'm frightened,' said Sidney.

'We'll be alright, Sidney, the moth seems to know what he's doing. Just hang on tight!'

As they grew closer Sidney could see that the other creatures were bright blue and slimy and were riding shiny black beetles. The large white moth flew into the beetle pack and blinded them with its brilliance. They fell away and the bats were able to bite them to bits. Some of the beetles got through and fought ferociously, bringing down some of the little grey creatures. The fight didn't last long though, and Sidney's friends won the battle and rode on into the red city, landing in front of the palace.

The moth fluttered down on to the courtyard.

A large blue slimy thing crawled out with its attendants from a golden door. It writhed and raged in temper. As Sidney approached it after dismounting from the moth, it spat sticky goo at him and stuck him to the floor. Rearing up, it lashed out at Sidney with its rasping tongue. Sidney wanted to run, but couldn't move. The moth could see the danger, and lifting himself towards the evil ruler, blinded him by flashing his silver wings. As he thrashed about on the floor, his attendants ran away in panic. The little grey creatures overran the palace and news got out to the slimy blue creatures who then stopped fighting.

Sidney managed to free himself from the sticky goo, and sat down to have a rest.

Something came looking for him in excitement.

'What is it?' said Sidney.

'The grey creatures have found a secret vault under the palace.'

'Right let's go and have a look,' said Sidney.

They ran through the large corridors of the palace to a staircase that led down into a deep dark place. 'How are we going to be able to see down there?' said Something.

'Ask moth if he would come and spread his wings,' said Sidney.

'Good idea, I'll fetch him.'

Moth spread out his wings and lit up the vault. Sidney could see a very old leather-bound book on a table next to a large crystal pyramid. He flipped over some thick pages and saw ancient writings and a drawing of this crystal with rainbows of colours coming from it. Sidney said to Something, 'The crystal has been put in the dark and a spell cast over the land.'

'Let's take the crystal into the courtyard then and see what happens,' said Something.

Sidney managed to get the little grey creatures to move the crystal up into the light, but nothing changed. The sky was still green and the city glowed red. Sidney was very disappointed, and walked away wondering what else he could possibly do to help. He wandered down one of the corridors and through an old wooden door which creaked and groaned itself shut after him. A strong gust of wind took Sidney across to the fireplace, where he steadied himself. He looked up and saw a stone sticking out further than the others with strange writing on it. While feeling across the carved words with his fingers, he heard a grinding noise coming from the fireplace. As he looked down into the blackened grate, a hole appeared at the back. Sidney squeezed through and, losing his footing, slipped backwards into the darkness. He landed with a bump at the bottom and saw a glow in the distance.

Sidney was scared, but continued along the tunnel into the pure white light where he saw many beautiful things. People with long silver hair, golden robes and very friendly faces, floated up to greet him.

One of them said to Sidney, 'Welcome to the Land of Rainbows, and don't be afraid. We know who you are and can help you with your quest.'

Sidney said, 'I found a crystal and took it into the light to try to change everything for the little grey creatures, but it didn't work against the evil force there.'

'There is a key to fit into the device and we can direct you to it, but you will have one more challenge to face, Sidney. We will give you a guide, and her name is Runa,' said one of the beautiful people.

'Oh thank you,' said Sidney, 'when can we start?'

'Have a rest for a while and something to eat and drink, and I will fetch Runa to meet you.'

Sidney sat and ate the most delicious cakes that he had ever tasted, and his drink sparkled with all the colours from the rainbow.

Runa came over to greet him and said that she was going to help him to find the crystal key.

She led him to a valley where two golden eagles were gliding around on the warm thermals. Runa whispered on the breeze to them and they answered by landing in front of her. She told Sidney to climb up and hang on to the eagle's feathered neck, then they took off and flew up high into the Mountains of Rainbows.

Sidney looked down and saw a light coming from the side of a glacier.

'Sidney, this is the place of colours and I shall ask my two friends to land on the icy ledge just over there, so hang on tight.'

As they landed the eagles skidded to a halt, Sidney went head over heels landing with a bump on the side of the mountain.

'Sidney, are you alright?' said Runa as she dismounted her eagle.

'Yes I'm fine.'

Runa whispered to her two friends again and they flew off.

'This is where we will find the crystal key. Let's go inside,' said Runa.

Sidney and Runa walked together into a large cave that was lit by some insects clinging to the walls. At one end there was a door carved out of stone. Sidney went over and touched it and it swung open revealing a dark room.

'Look out, Sidney,' said Runa, but Sidney was too slow. Two giant green eyes stared at him from the darkness, and a clawed hand grabbed at him, whisking him up into the air. He landed inside a large mouth with yellow teeth and a dripping red tongue.

Sidney was frightened but, remembering some words he'd read in the leather-bound book, he yelled the spell out loud and the evil monster vanished, dropping him onto the floor with a bump. 'That was horrible, Runa, I thought he was going to eat me,' said Sidney.

Runa saw the crystal key hanging up near the stone door. She lifted it off very carefully and said, 'Sidney, let's go home, we have the key.' She whispered on the wind and the eagles came to her.

Sidney and Runa mounted them and flew back to the people in the Land of Rainbows.

They were overjoyed to have Runa back and gave a great feast for Sidney. When the party had finished, Sidney waved goodbye to everyone. Holding on to the crystal key, he closed his eyes.

When he opened them again he was standing by the crystal in the palace courtyard.

'It's good to see you again Sidney, we have missed you,' said Something from Somewhere.

'I have the key to the crystal that will drive all the evil forces away, and change the planet back to how it was,' said Sidney.

As he inserted the crystal key into a slot in the side, there was a terrific bolt of lightning and a crash of thunder. A cascade of coloured light fell down like rain on to everything, changing the evil red landscape back into a beautiful place. The little grey creatures were delighted and thanked Sidney and Something for all their help. Sidney shut his eyes and wished he was back at home, and, as he slowly opened them again, found that he really was.

'What an adventure Sidney,' said Something.

'Yes, Something, by helping the little grey creatures, we found the key to solving the mystery.'

Annabelle's Cloud Nine

Hazel Brydon

'Annabelle, Annabelle! Do hurry up and come now, it's time for the fireworks! Daddy has started the bonfire, oh, do come on!'

Annabelle rubbed drowsy blue eyes and shook her fair curls as her little brother tugged impatiently at her arm.

The children had been looking forward all week to this moment. It was November 5th and Ben's birthday.

They knew of course that it isn't wise to play with matches and fireworks without adult supervision. Daddy said it could be quite dangerous.

Annabelle's heart filled with excitement as she scrambled from the big bed in Mummy's room where she had sat reading.

'Alright, alright! I'm coming, don't be so impatient Ben, you know it's silly to rush.' She was really repeating what her mother always taught them.

She followed Ben out into the garden. It was almost dark now. Soon the sky would come alive with the rosy glow from the fire heaped high with wood and other rubbish carefully collected for the big day.

All their friends were watching as orange tongues of flame began to leap higher and higher 'midst the twirls of curling grey smoke. What a wonderful sight it was. Soon Mother would appear with steaming mugs of cocoa and hot jacketed potatoes.

Suddenly Annabelle's attention was caught by what appeared to be some huge object standing alone in a shadowy corner of the garden.

She wandered over to see what it might be. It was some kind of rocket, she thought. It really looked like a giant sized firework, covered with bright blue and yellow paper it even had an extra bright orange taper right at the end of its nose.

She noticed that it stood horizontally on a small stand which was only just the right size to hold it. *Perhaps it's a present for Ben*, she thought, and was just about to skip over to her parents to ask when she noticed a small ladder attached to the side.

The steps led from the ground right up to the top and just above them was a little seat.

Curiosity got the better of her judgement then, she really couldn't resist climbing up to take a closer look.

As she did so she noticed some large letters printed on the side of the large object.

'*Do not light me*' said the words as she read them. Annabelle laughed out loud, *as if anyone would dare put a match to a firework this size,* she thought. *The bang would frighten half the neighbourhood.*

She found the tiny seat to be quite comfortable and settled herself into it. From here she could look down upon the garden scene below.

Already brilliant streaks of red, green and silver were searing through the skies as Daddy took charge of the display. Annabelle decided to join the others.

Just at that very moment a spark from the now enormous bonfire slowly fluttered down and rested upon the orange taper and before Annabelle could hastily scramble down the ladder there was a great *whoosh!* followed by a loud *bang!* as the taper sprang into flames and off shot the rocket with poor Annabelle clinging tightly on as best she could.

'Oooh help!' squealed Annabelle, 'oooh! Whatever shall I do now?' Yet curiously enough she didn't feel at all frightened as the giant rocket soared away into the night.

Once the shock had worn off, she found it quite pleasant to be drifting through the night air close to the velvety sky.

A gentle peaceful sense of 'well being' surged through her even as she looked down to see the garden and the red glowing bonfire slowly receding into the distance.

'They will wonder where I've gone,' she sighed, 'I do hope Mummy and Daddy won't be cross that I left so suddenly.' But right now nothing seemed important anymore.

Adjusting herself to the billowing night air as the rocket rose higher, Annabelle tried to peer through the gloom to see where she was heading.

I do hope it's somewhere nice, she thought.

Presently she noticed a huge white cloud looming up in the distance.

'I wonder whether we shall pass through that or over it,' she muttered to herself, feeling just a little nervous at the idea.

The cloud seemed to be shaped into a figure nine, and, just as she noticed that, the rocket nose-dived right into the midst of it.

Annabelle was conscious of a hard little bump as she was landed on what appeared quite solid ground.

She was more than a little bewildered now. Everywhere seemed to be thick with mist. Climbing from her seat she felt her way down the small ladder still attached to the side.

She could just make out the words printed on the side, they had changed. They now said *'Return to Earth by midnight'*.

Well at least I shall have time to look around, she thought, as she foraged her way through the mist.

Presently the atmosphere cleared and she came to a high building which appeared half tower, half fairy castle.

It seemed to be built up of fabric in all the colours of the rainbow. Not like the buildings she knew at all.

Cautiously she made her way to the entrance. This was blocked by an enormous purple boulder of cloud which simply rolled away as she approached.

Peering carefully through the opening her eyes were dazzled by the sheer beauty they beheld.

The walls seemed to be formed from brightly polished diamonds which shimmered and sparkled whilst colourfully reflecting the light and the rainbowed walls outside.

The ceiling hung low with gold spun spider webbing, each intricate pattern glinting and gleaming brightly.

Annabelle caught her breath sharply, she had never seen anything like this in her whole life. Even the floors seemed to be of clear still blue water until she put one foot tentatively forward to test the ground.

Plucking up all her courage she walked in.

How exciting it all was! She walked slowly over the blue floor. Presently she noticed a small round door in the diamond wall. Annabelle decided to knock.

'Come in,' called a croaky voice. The door opened all by itself. Annabelle peered cautiously around the edge. The room had the same sparkly walls and ceiling but the floor was different. She noticed that it appeared lumpy brown like earth, with green patches here and there. *Just like soil and grass*, she thought.

'Well, don't just stand there! Come in!' cried the voice. She walked forward very slowly. There was no one to be seen.

Just then a beautiful orange moon beamed his way smilingly into the room through the icicles at the window. The room came alive with light and Annabelle saw that the stars were now filling the skies outside with a myriad of tiny green and yellow glowing lamps. *It must be getting near to midnight,* she thought anxiously.

'I'm very sorry to bother you,' she called out politely to the invisible voice. 'But I saw this door and thought someone might help me to know where I am.'

'Aah! Yes!' came the reply, 'humans are always doing it, they light up the tapers and then wonder why they arrive here.'

'I didn't mean to,' explained Annabelle. 'It was a spark from the fire, not me.'

'Yes, yes!' the voice sounded irritable, 'but you were meddling you see! You shouldn't have been on the rocket in the first place.'

Annabelle blushed. She had meddled with her brother's present. 'I thought it was a gift for Ben, I only wanted to look.'

'Well it wasn't,' the exasperated voice replied, it was an experiment. It was sent to test the amount of meddling that goes on among humans. They meddle with this, and meddle with that you know. Human beings are only happy when they are meddling.'

Just then another door opened and suddenly the room was filled with birds! They were the largest crowd of the most lovely birds that Annabelle could ever wish to see.

There were scarlet birds and green birds, pink ones and blue ones, blackbirds and white doves, brown sparrows and thrushes, orange and yellow birds. All were sweetly singing, all wore crowns of gold and silver and each had a precious gem set in the centre of its forehead.

Annabelle was speechless. They surrounded her and gazed upon her, their glittering eyes gleaming from their very wise old faces.

At last she found her tongue again and addressed the leader, a large golden eagle. The one with the croaky voice. 'How beautiful you all are,' she cried.

'That's because we are not meddled with,' he retorted. He drew out a large pair of spectacles from under his feathered wing. Placing them between his sharp eyes and his beak he stared at Annabelle, who began to feel a very insignificant creature indeed.

She heard from him all about the beautiful places hidden among the clouds and of lovely other worlds about which humans know little. Places where sick and suffering birds and animals are often taken to recover from cruel treatment on Earth.

'Human beings must learn to be kinder to animals and to plants,' explained the wise old eagle. 'They too have to live and grow, flowers blossom more beautifully when they are loved.'

Annabelle felt she understood now what he meant by meddling humans! She resolved to be extra kind in future to all her pets and the plants that Daddy grew in the garden too.

'Please tell me, Sir,' she asked the eagle, 'one thing puzzles me, why is it that the icicles don't melt, it is so warm in here.'

The old bird smiled at her, and all the other birds began to sing and move their wings in rhythm to the sound.

'Why, bless my soul dear child . . . don't you know? It is because this room is filled with *love*,' he spread out his giant wings as though to cover all within.

'*Love* is the secret, love is our sunshine and love is our nourishment. We could not exist without love and everything that ever was exists because of it.'

Annabelle thought very deeply about this, she would tell everyone when she got back to Earth.

'Well, we have enjoyed your visit,' said the wise old bird, happy now that he had made her understand, 'but you must hurry away, it is almost midnight!'

'Oh yes! I must!' cried Annabelle, 'but there is no taper left to light on the rocket,' she said anxiously.

'That's because you meddled,' muttered the eagle returning to his severe voice.

However she need not have worried, the birds carried her off on their strong wings and in no time at all she was back safely at home.

'Wake up! Do wake up!' Annabelle jumped with the sound of his voice. Benny had come to call her into the garden. 'Wake up sleepyhead,' he cried, 'it's time to start the fireworks!'

Aimée And Jack In London

Janet Granger

Victoria was so excited travelling to London on the train with her mummy. The weather was warm and sunny and today was her fourth birthday. Tucking into a sandwich, Victoria gazed out of the window at the sheep in the fields. 'Do we get off at the next station, Mummy?'
'Two more stops dear, it won't be long now.'
'Did you hear that Aimée?' Victoria whispered to Aimée, her doll, sitting close to her. 'We are going to have a lovely day, shopping in London, and buy a new dress for me, and one for you.'
'Pack up your lunch bags Victoria and put them into the waste bin,' said Victoria's mummy. 'We will soon be arriving at the station, and make sure Aimée is tucked under your arm.'
The train slowed down and then came to a halt. Victoria's mummy pressed the button which opened the train door. 'Hold my hand Victoria, there's a gap between the train and the platform.'
Victoria felt very small hurrying along amongst all the people. She remembered how to insert her ticket into the machine, which opened the barrier.
Outside the station, buses and taxis were waiting.
'There's a bus over there Victoria, it's going to Oxford Street, so we'll hop on that one.'
'Can we sit upstairs, Mummy, we may see the Queen's palace and the guards?' asked Victoria.
It was so exciting, spending a day in London. The noise of the traffic and people walking hurriedly in all directions.
They had settled upstairs on the bus, when Victoria's mummy said, 'Victoria, where's Aimée?'
'Oh,' said Victoria, looking worried, 'I don't know. I was holding her when I got off the train.'
'Then you must have dropped her. We will have to enquire at the station before boarding the train home.'
'Poor Aimée,' whimpered Victoria, wiping a tear away, 'she will be frightened on her own without me.'

Aimée was frightened. She had been dropped onto the platform amongst the bustle of people walking quickly. *Any moment now*, she thought, *I will be trodden on.*

She opened her eyes and looked up to see an old lady bending down to pick her up.

'Oh, you poor little thing,' she said, 'some little girl will be missing you. I'll take you to the lost property office.'

The attendant put Aimée into a wire basket. The basket was filled with handbags, scarves, gloves, umbrellas, but no other toys or dolls.

Aimée waited patiently, hoping Victoria would remember where she dropped her and come looking for her. Then suddenly, something was thrown almost on top of her.

'Look out,' Aimée cried angrily, 'you will crumple my dress!'

Two large amber eyes stared back at her.

'Oh,' she said, 'you're a teddy bear, and a scruffy one at that! What's your name?'

'My name's Jack,' said the teddy bear quietly.

'That's a funny name for a teddy,' said Aimée. 'Are you lost too?'

'Yes,' replied Jack, 'I was left on the train by my Thomas. He's just had his birthday, and he's four years old.'

'Well,' said Aimée, 'we can keep one another company until they come to collect us. I hope it won't be too long. I don't like it here. Victoria dropped me on the platform. We were going to spend a day in London for her birthday treat. I live by the seaside and my name is Aimée. Where do you live Jack?'

'I live in an old farm house, surrounded by fields. We have chickens and ducks, rabbits, a horse, a goat and an old donkey. Oh, and two dogs and two cats.' Jack hoped he would soon be home with his family.

'We don't have any animals at all,' declared Aimée. 'Have you been lost before, Jack?'

'Yes,' frowned Jack, 'sometimes Tom leaves me at play school all night, and other times he forgets to take me, so I get left next to his muddy boots in the kitchen, but I don't mind.'

'Do you have clean clothes on every day, Jack?' asked Aimée. 'I do. Victoria has long blonde hair, the same as me, and at night, she brushes her hair and then mine. In the morning, I always have a clean dress and socks. Then she puts on my black shiny shoes.'

'I've had this red jumper on for three weeks,' said Jack, 'and it needs stitching. I've got holes in the elbows. Tom carries me all round the farmyard, so we both get muddy.'

Aimée began to cry. 'I shall be scared if I have to stay here all night. I've got my own bed at home, next to Victoria's bed.'

'Never mind,' said Jack bravely, 'I will look after you.'

'Thank you Jack,' sobbed Aimée, 'you might look a bit scruffy, but you are very kind. Will you be my friend?'

'Of course,' replied Jack.

The door opened and the attendant walked in. He began to sweep the floor with a special large mop. He looked into the basket. 'Are you two still here?' he exclaimed.

Jack and Aimée stayed still and quiet. They never let people know they could talk to one another.

When the attendant left, Aimée turned to Jack. 'It must be getting dark now. It seems we have been here a long time.'

The door opened again, and there stood Victoria and her mummy and, to Jack's amazement, right behind them was Thomas and his mummy. They were talking as if they knew one another. Thomas was inviting Victoria to play at his house one day.

'There's Aimée,' cried Victoria, snatching her up into her arms, 'I thought I would never see you again.'

Aimée was so pleased to see Victoria. She peeped from under Victoria's arm and whispered, 'Goodbye, Jack, thank you for being my friend. I hope one day, we will meet again.'

'Yes,' sighed Jack, sad to see Aimée go, 'so do I.'

Katie And The Little Owl Return To The Magic Wood

Christine Hardemon

It was a warm July evening, the sort you don't often get in midsummer, and the evening air brought the scent of the flowers to Katie's nose. She was playing in her garden, the school holidays had just started and she had six weeks to keep herself occupied. What was she going to do? She didn't have any pets to look after and keep her busy. She had often asked her parents for a pet but they had so far refused saying 'you are not old enough to look after any animal yet' and 'when you get bigger we shall see' and all the time she was getting bigger and older and still no sign of any pet! She sighed! What could she do? What pet would she like, a dog, a cat, a hamster and then she suddenly thought of her friend Little Owl. He would be a great companion, but where was he? She hadn't seen him for ages.

Katie began to feel very sad. The last time they met he said it might be their last adventure as he was getting quiet old. She probably wouldn't see him again, and she was just about to start crying when she heard her father's voice calling her.

'Katie, where are you? There you are,' he said, 'I've been calling you and you didn't hear me, it's such a lovely evening, Mum and I thought that we would take you and Sam to the funfair which has just arrived on the village green. Would you like to go? Sam and Mum are waiting, come on.' Without waiting for a reply, he took her hand and off they went.

Sam was Katie's brother, he wasn't much older than her, but he tried to be grown-up and was allowed to stay up longer than her at the weekends. He was also allowed to have a pet hamster and Katie thought this most unfair. Never mind, she would still 'work' on her parents this summer holiday to try and get their permission to have a pet of some sort, perhaps a rabbit or a guinea pig.

Katie and her dad soon caught up with Sam and her mum and they walked along the country lanes to the village green.

When they arrived several of Katie's friends were there with their parents. Katie called out and waved to them as they passed. She then decided which rides she would like to go on.

'They all looked very scary,' said Sam, 'some of them are so high.'

Not half as high as when I flew with Little Owl, thought Katie to herself and gave a smug grin.

'What are you grinning at?' asked Sam.

Katie did not reply.

After a wonderful evening it was soon time to go home and at last Katie felt she must go to bed as she was so tired. So when her mum and dad told her and Sam it was time to go, neither Katie nor Sam argued.

Katie fell into bed dreaming about the funfair and slowly drifted off to sleep.

Next day it was raining and Katie was so glad they had gone to the funfair the evening before. If this amount of rain kept up the ground would be so muddy and wet. Pity anyone who had arranged to go tonight.

She had her breakfast and then went into her toy room to look for something to play with. As she did so she glanced out of the corner of her eye at something sitting in the corner of the room. It wasn't any of her toys - it was Little Owl.

Katie's heart thumped with delight, Little Owl had come to visit her again and she wondered whether another adventure was about to begin.

Little Owl spoke to Katie in his gentle way and told her that he had been staying in the Magic Wood with Crocus, Petal, Bluebell and all the other fairies and pixies. However the wood was now in danger of being cleared to make way for a housing development and all the fairies and pixies were very frightened.

Little Owl was just about to ask for Katie's help when the toy room door burst open and in came her brother Sam. When he saw Little Owl he stopped in amazement at the sight of an owl sitting in the room. The next moment he was even more astonished when Little Owl started to speak. Sam's jaw fell open and his mouth grew wider in surprise.

'Oh,' said Katie to her brother, 'let me introduce you to my friend Little Owl.'

Sam was speechless and sat down with Katie and Little Owl on the floor. Katie explained that this was a very big secret and he must promise not to tell any of his friends about Little Owl.

Sam did not believe her at first when she told him about the adventures that she had with Little Owl, about the Magic Wood, the Mermaid Queen, oh, and also her visit to Father Christmas. Sam was so sure she was making up all these stories so he said to her, 'Go on, prove it, I really don't believe a word you are saying.'

Then Little Owl spoke in his gentle way and said, 'As you are Katie's brother I am going to ask you and Katie if you would help me and all the fairies who live in the Magic Wood.'

At once Katie said they would. Sam was as excited as Katie had been the first time she met Little Owl and yelled, 'Come on, let's go!'

Well of course to be able to fly with Little Owl they had to shrink to a very small size and Katie explained to Sam that he had to close his eyes whilst Little Owl's wings were put around him. Sam agreed and soon he and Katie were Little Owl's size and climbing onto his back, just as Katie had done before when she had been to visit the fairies and pixies.

It was a bit of a squeeze for Katie and Sam but they hung on to each other as Little Owl made his way up in the sky. It was very wet and windy, but the wind helped blow them on their way as it was blowing the way in which they wanted to fly.

Soon they were whizzing through the sky and over very high treetops. Katie knew the Magic Wood was getting closer as she could see the golden leaves of the trees ahead.

They landed in a clearing in the Magic Wood. Sam was astonished at the beauty of the wood and felt sad to think that this was going to be cleared because of a housing estate. He knew people had to live somewhere, but why couldn't they put buildings up to replace older buildings that were falling down instead of using up more of the countryside.

Katie spoke and broke Sam's thoughts by saying, 'Look over there Sam, can you see the muntjac deer having its lunch and oh look it has a baby.'

Katie, Sam and Little Owl rested for a while whilst watching the animals in the Magic Wood, and then Little Owl said they must be on their way. They climbed on his back and very slowly he rose into the air, the journey further into the wood was rather slower than before, as Little Owl was now beginning to feel tired with the weight of both Katie and her brother. He was glad when they finally reached the golden cottage. It was still surrounded by pretty flowers, but Katie noticed that because it was later in the summer there seemed to be even more flowers making it look more beautiful than ever.

'Open the latch, Katie,' called Little Owl.

So as before Katie pushed the door and pushed very hard, her brother Sam helped and was shocked at the sight that met his eyes.

'Welcome,' said Katie, 'to Fairyland.'

The children, along with Little Owl, walked on through the door and then down the winding path to the fairies' homes. It was just how Katie remembered, with all the toadstools looking so neat and tidy - even Petal's home was spick and span. Katie thought how different it looked the last time she came when it was all a mess. Now it was sparkling like all the rest of the little homes.

Katie spotted Petal outside her home tidying up the garden. Petal screamed with delight when she saw Katie. On hearing her scream all the other pixies and fairies came rushing out of their homes to greet the friends. Katie explained that she and her brother were there to help everyone. Katie introduced Sam to each of the fairies and pixies in turn and the trio were then invited to each of the little homes. *It would be so sad to have all these little homes destroyed,* thought Katie, *but what could they do?*

Soon everybody was chatting and enjoying the food that the fairies had brought. Katie, Sam and Little Owl were famished after their journey, but it wasn't long before they felt better and were soon discussing what they could do to help. They were talking so loud and excitedly that they didn't hear the rumbling noise in the distance, until Little Owl said, 'Listen, is that the sound of machinery that I can hear - have they started to destroy the wood already?'

Everybody started to panic, including Katie and Sam. They hadn't even thought of a plan yet. The fairies started to cry - Bluebell, Petal and Crocus were in floods of tears. The pixies tried to comfort them. Suddenly Katie had a marvellous idea. 'I know,' she cried, 'you can all come and live with Sam and me in our garden - it's quite big and there is plenty of room for everyone.'

The pixies, fairies and Little Owl thought that this was a fantastic idea and soon they were rushing around gathering any small thing they might want to take. Of course they would have to build new homes, but at least they would be safe from the machinery.

Very soon everyone gathered round with their belongings, and Katie and Sam climbed onto Little Owl's back - but the journey to the Magic Wood had been a difficult one for Little Owl and he was very tired. He tried to take off the ground, but he just couldn't with the weight of the children. He fell back onto the ground exhausted. Katie and Sam scrambled from his back and rushed to get him some water. The fairies were all looking on - the plan seemed doomed now. Then Bluebell said, 'If Little Owl can't carry you both on his back then all of us fairies and pixies will help. Hold our hands Katie and Sam.'

So they all gathered around and held hands. The fairies gently lifted off the ground with Katie and Sam holding tightly. Little Owl, now recovered after taking a drink of water, was able to fly without Katie and Sam's weight on his back.

It was sad leaving the Magic Wood behind, but they knew that it was not the place to be now that the men with the machinery were there. Katie and Sam looked sadly down as they held the fairies' hands and Little Owl followed them into the sky.

At long last they reached the children's home and Katie directed them to the top end of their garden. The fairies and pixies were delighted when they saw the place which was to be their new home. There was only one thing left for Little Owl to do now and that was to return Katie and Sam to their normal size. Katie and Sam both closed their eyes and Little Owl used his last bit of magic by putting his wings round them both. Now they were bigger than Little Owl, and he looked so small and frail.

Katie said to Little Owl, 'You can stay in our garden too, along with the fairies and pixies.'

Little Owl was delighted. He felt that his days of adventures were over and he needed a rest. He flew to the top of a tree and hooted down - then he drifted off to sleep.

That night when Katie was tucked up in bed she heard the 'twit-twoo' of Little Owl and she smiled. The fairies and pixies were in her garden and Little Owl was hooting in the tree. She had no need of a pet now. She had Little Owl - her very own dear friend who was going to stay with her forever.

The Dragon's Tale
(For Troy)

Emma Lockyer

Once upon a time, a long, long time ago, in a faraway place called China, lived a dragon called Xing (pronounced Zing). Now Xing was not an ordinary dragon, he was a fire dragon. Fire dragons have many colours and Xing was no exception, in fact he had every colour of the rainbow on different parts of his body. Although Xing was a fire dragon, he lived in the mountains overlooking a small village, and on some evenings he would blow fire and turn the sky into different colours, sometimes red and yellow, sometimes a deep gold and purple.

The villagers liked the different colours that Xing could bring to the sky, so one day a man called Chan wondered if he could make his own colours in the sky. Chan was a metalsmith by trade and he noticed that when he burned certain metals in the fire he could see different colours.

One day, Chan was working in his shop when he was visited by Soong, a gunsmith, who had come to ask him if he had any metal bands to bind a rifle. Chan was making a kettle and the piece of metal he was using turned blue, not just any blue, but a deep, bright blue, brighter than the ocean. Chan showed Soong the colour of the metal in his fire, Soong admitted that he liked the colour too. He had never seen anything like that before, it almost reminded him of Xing, the dragon. The two men sat down for a cup of tea and pondered how to get the colour deepest blue in the sky. It would be one of the most beautiful sights, like watching Xing fly, although he did not do this very often.

The next day Chan and Soong decided to try and see what they could do in Soong's workshop. Chan bought some more metals, while Soong found a small pot and half filled it with gunpowder. Chan then put some of the metal dust into the pot. Soong laid a fuse wire from the pot and lit the other end, then carried it outside for safety, placing it on the ground. Chan and Soong stood well back and waited. The pot exploded but the gunpowder had set fire to the metal dust and it fell like fairy dust, red, silver and blue fluttering in the afternoon breeze. Chan and Soong stood there open mouthed, even the villagers that had heard the sound came running to see what had happened, catching the tail end of the spectacle. Soon Chan and Soong were asked to repeat the fiery lights, and so they set to work using different metals and different combinations.

Chan and Soong continued working into the early evening. As it got darker and darker, so the fire-worked lights became brighter and brighter until the lights reached far into the dark sky. Even the explosions got bigger and bigger as the villagers wanted to see more and more displays.

Xing opened one eye. He had just heard a big bang, followed by other even bigger bangs. He lifted his head and noticed the glow in the sky that came with the big bangs. He stood up and walked a little further around his cave and there below him was the most spectacular of sights. He sat down to await the end. As the morning light came across the sky, the fiery lights ended. Xing went back to sleep and dreamed of the bright lights.

Chan and Soong had run out of the metals and the gunpowder needed to create the fiery lights, but they had enough orders from the villagers to keep them busy for a whole year, so they set off to the coast to buy loads more supplies. Xing wanted to see more of the bright lights and decided to go down into the village and see what was going on. As he got closer, he could hear the villagers talking about the great fiery lights. Xing listened.

'Chan has decided that he should use rockets to get the lights into the sky,' an old man said.

'Soong wants to use whistles, and spin them on a nail,' said the other old man.

Xing was intrigued, rockets and whistles. He would like to see this, so he lay low in the bushes and waited.

That evening Chan and Soong returned with a huge wagonload full of the things that they needed and set about putting them into Chan's workshop, because his workshop was biggest. When they had finished they decided after all of their hard work they would go to sleep and begin making the next batch of fiery lights in the morning.

Xing had fallen asleep, but was awoken by a popping sound. Chan's workshop was on fire! Xing sat up, some of the gunpowder was beginning to burn, then there was a series of explosions. Xing was afraid. He blew on the workshop, but the flames grew higher and higher. Xing roared and when the villagers heard his roar, they saw the fire and immediately set about putting buckets of water over it. Xing dug up the soil using his hind legs, spraying the fire with sand. Chan and Soong came running, just in time to see the villagers and Xing putting out the last of the fire.

Chan and Soong checked the workshop for damage. Fortunately most of the gunpowder was untouched, safe in the fireproof sacks. Only the powder that had been opened the night before had gone, and there was very little of that left to begin with. Chan and Soong were relieved. The villagers and Xing had saved almost everything.

Xing was invited to a spectacular display of fiery lights. The Emperor of China had heard of the strange spectacular, and people in the nearby towns had also seen or heard about it. The Emperor jumped when he heard the loud bangs and put his fingers in his ears when he heard the whistles. He cheered when he saw the huge array of colours in the night sky. At the end of the display, the Emperor presented Chan and Soong with a silk shirt each, and on the back was an embroidery of Xing the dragon. He also gave them a huge order of fiery lights for his birthday. The Emperor gave Xing a huge black pearl as a big thank you for helping to save the workshop, all of the villagers cheered, waving the flags and paper models of Xing that they had made for the occasion.

Findel's Apprentice - Elves And Dragons

Josephine Carter

Brom was cutting wood outside Findel's house, which lay in the forest of Trewella. The early morning mist was lifting, broken by the sun's warmth. 'I am so glad Findel feels much better now. Destroying the Wild Magic certainly put a strain on him,' Brom told Tarrow, who was sitting on the grass watching his friend.

'Yes, I think it was not good for any of us. I am glad it's over. Has Findel told you how to call the Dragons yet?'

Brom shook his head, 'No I still don't know how to call them to me, but I know Findel will tell me when he is ready.'

Brom had told Tarrow that he and Findel were going to the High Stone. No one had ever asked him to go with them to such a place before. He felt excited and pleased. All sorts of things pleased him, especially anything to do with his best friend, Brom. This day was going to be special.

With the last log cut ready for the wood-stack, Brom put away his axe. He and Tarrow then made their way to Findel's house. They found Findel sitting by the window. He was reading his old battered spell book. His half-moon glasses had slipped down to the end of his long nose. 'There you are Brom, are you ready for today's lesson?' Findel asked.

'Yes I am, I have asked Tarrow to come with us, I hope this is all right with you.' Brom gave Findel one of his innocent smiles and Findel said that Tarrow could come as long as he kept out of the way.

Findel often sounded harsh, but all who knew the old wizard said his bark was worse than his bite. This was very true, so Tarrow knew he was welcome to go with them.

Findel rose from his chair, tucked his spell book under his arm and left his house. Brom and Tarrow followed, they talked incessantly.

'Be quiet you two,' the wizard shouted.

'We are sorry Findel, it will not happen again,' said the two friends together. They looked at each other trying hard not to laugh, but sounds of spluttering came out of their mouths.

Findel stopped and turned to face them. 'If you cannot behave together, then Tarrow will have to go back. Well, what do you say?' asked the wizard.

'We will do as you say Findel, we are sorry,' replied Brom.

Tarrow did not say anything, just looked down at the ground. He did not want to go home. At last they came upon the High Stone.

'I did not dream it could be so grand,' Tarrow told Brom.

The wizard walked towards the grey stone, markings were ground onto the smooth face of the stone. 'Come along Brom, I have much to teach you.'

Brom left Tarrow, he was still enthralled by the appearance of the magic stone. The apprentice moved to his teacher's side. 'I am ready, Findel,' he said.

Findel told him to repeat the words that were on the stone. 'You must not falter, speak loud and clear,' the wizard gold him.

Brom spoke the words. As he did so, Brom began to vanish. Tarrow could not believe it, this was great magic and it could be useful too.

'Right Brom, you must say the words backwards to reappear,' Findel said to the empty space that had been Brom. No answer came. 'Brom, answer me,' demanded Findel. Still no answer came. Now the wizard became worried, so too was Tarrow. He shouted for his friend to come back, but still no Brom.

'Ho that silly boy, I know what has happened,' Findel told Tarrow, shaking his head. 'He has said the invisible word at the end of the escape spell, and has passed into the secret land of the elves.'

Tarrow looked worried. 'What will happen to Brom, will he be all right in the elvish lands?' he asked the old wizard.

Findel pulled Tarrow towards the High Stone. 'Do not worry so,' Findel told him, 'together we will find Brom and you will get to see the elves of old.'

Just as Brom had vanished, so did Findel and Tarrow. They reappeared in a very different place, it was an elvish village. Tarrow had never seen the like, golden towers stood tall among the trees, and soft, serene music drifted on warm breezes. 'Look, over there, it's Brom,' said Tarrow feeling quite overwhelmed. 'Brom, Brom,' he shouted.

'Hush, you do not raise your voice here,' Findel told him in a very strict voice. Findel walked over to where Brom was standing. He was deep in conversation with a tall and elegant elf. The elf wore a tunic of sky blue and his long hair was the colour of spun gold. 'Brom, what have you done? You are not supposed to be here, not here in this village!' said Findel angrily.

'Do not worry yourself Findel, this young wizard looked deep and saw our secret word. We welcome him as an elf friend, such as you are,' the tall elf told Findel.

'Thank you for being so understanding Telmar, he is but my apprentice and so young.'

The elves bade them stay. Tarrow could not believe his good fortune, if it had not been for the escape spell going wrong he would never have met the elves. After feasting and the singing of songs, Findel told Telmar that he had to return his charges to the forest of Trewella.

'Go in peace my friends, and I hope we will meet again. I have a gift for you Brom, guard it well, for one day you may need our help.' The tall elf gave Brom a horn, it was very beautiful. It was ringed in silver, engraved with ancient elvish words. 'Blow but once upon this horn and we will come to your aid,' said Telmar.

Brom thanked him and bade all the elves goodbye.

Once back in the forest, Brom and Tarrow looked at the horn. 'It is crafted perfectly Brom, I wish it were mine,' Tarrow told him.

'I will keep this gift with me for all time.' He hung it over his shoulder, where it would stay forever.

'Well, Findel, have you any other lessons as interesting as the last one?' Brom asked.

Findel looked at Brom's innocent smile. 'Come Tarrow,' Findel said, 'I think I shall teach you the Dragon Spell.' Findel smiled and Tarrow looked afraid. 'I am only jesting, Tarrow,' laughed the wizard. Brom laughed too. 'Well Brom, would you like to call a dragon?' asked Findel.

'Yes, ho yes, I would. But just a small one to start with,' Brom replied.

Findel whispered the spell into Brom's ear and then told him to go to the clearing and call the dragon.

Brom left Findel and Tarrow, he felt excited, but also afraid. He had never met a dragon before. In the clearing Brom called the spell out loud and waited. He did not have to wait long, he looked up and there in the sky above him, a dragon descended.

On the ground the dragon bowed his head. The dragon's scales were green and red, they shimmered in the sunlight. At once Brom loved this fine creature. 'Good day, fine fellow,' said Brom. 'May I sit on your back?' he asked politely.

The dragon's red eyes twinkled, he bowed his head once more. Brom climbed upon its back, large wings appeared each side of its thick body, then the dragon flew upwards, the large wings flapping slowly. Brom held tight and below him he saw Findel and Tarrow waving to him. Once more the dragon circled then landed in the clearing.

'Thank you. If I need you, may I call on you again?' asked Brom.

For the last time the dragon bowed his head, then disappeared as if he had never existed.

'Thank you Findel,' Brom said breathlessly as he ran up to the wizard.

'Take care not to call them too often, they are apt to get very irritable,' Findel said laughing loudly. 'Now home for tea.'

'Today has been grand,' said Tarrow, 'but it has made me feel so hungry.'

'So Tarrow, you do not want to be an apprentice and learn spells?' Findel asked as they walked home.

'No way, I am glad to be Brom's friend, but never a wizard. Let's leave everything as it is.'

They laughed all the way back home.

Yes, it really was a good life, thought Brom, and he hoped to see again the new friends he had met today. He was certain he would.

Stolen Magic

Sam Denniss

Uncle Rick and Aunt Bess had been like parents to me. As a child I was always at their little cottage in Outer Harmsway. Uncle Rick thought it a great joke that Aunt Bess wanted them to be 'out of harm's way', I still chuckle when I see the signpost. I've not been back there for a long time now, I'm too busy touring like my uncle did. Let me tell you the story from the beginning.

Uncle Rick had been a successful magician who had toured the States. He never made a name for himself in England, but when he retired he came back to live in the village. Aunt Bess was a skilled seamstress who made the outfits they wore on stage. As a child I was spellbound by the acts he would put on for Trevor and me. Trevor was his son, a few years older than me; he never had the same enthusiasm for magic as I did. I sometimes feel guilty that perhaps I had replaced him as the son that Uncle Rick would really have liked. Maybe all the touring had soured him, but I used to call him Tricky Trev. He hated it, but as he was more into trickery than magic I felt it was an apt name.

Anyway, I was fascinated by Uncle Rick's magic. It wasn't just the tricks he did, it was the whole thing. He'd stand there in his magnificent coat and tails (packed with hidden devices and pockets) and his bright red gloves. His fox gloves, he called them, after the red foxgloves Aunt Bess grew in their cottage garden. With them he worked the amazing sleight of hand that a magician needs to persuade the audience that it's real magic. No matter what others may say, it is real magic. Not that we do the impossible, but we make people believe we can.

'Mickey,' he'd say, 'you must believe you are able to do real magic yourself, or no one else will believe you can.' That was after he started to show me how his magic worked. To start with I was just an enthralled and enthusiastic audience, clapping my hands in boyish delight, while Trev sat next to me with a surly face. When one day I looked my uncle in the eye and declared that I too wanted to be a magician and asked him to teach me, his face lit up. I can still see him laughing with delight.

'Mickey,' he announced, 'the Sorcerer's Apprentice.'

He was a very patient teacher and always encouraged and waited while I mastered the complex movements I needed to deceive the eye. I marvelled at all his magical equipment. He'd made everything himself. The centrepiece was his magic case from which he took his wands and baubles to dazzle and deceive. It bristled with secret compartments. In my teens he encouraged me to put on my own magic shows, firstly just for him and Aunt Bess and then for the schoolchildren in the village hall. I loved it and I loved them.

The last time I saw Uncle Rick, he invited me into his magic den and said he had something he needed to talk to me about. With great solemnity, befitting a great magician, he told me he was finally leaving the stage of life and wanted a magician worthy of his own greatness to follow him. After waving his wand across the room which housed all his apparatus, he declared that he was leaving it all to me and handed me the wand.

'But what about Trev?' I asked, even though I knew that shortly after reaching sixteen, Trev had long departed the cosy cottage and sought much less wonderful treasures than the magic his father had to offer.

'He's had more than enough, Mickey,' he shook his head sadly. 'More than enough.'

I knew that Uncle had bailed him out of gambling debts so I didn't feel too bad. In any case, what would Trev want with all that magic stuff?

'Humour me son, just show me you know how to open the special compartment of my box.'

This was the trickiest thing Uncle Rick had ever taught me, the secret compartment at the bottom of his magic box was the hardest to master.

'Of course, Uncle. Presto Digitator,' I announced and waved the wand, tapping the place I knew with just the right touch to release it. The compartment fell open and several bundles of one hundred dollar bills fell to the floor. There were many more inside.

'A little I saved from my tours,' Uncle Rick said, as I stood with my mouth open.

'We want you to have it all,' said Aunt Bess. She had entered silently and was standing by the door. 'And Mickey, I hope you don't mind humouring me, but I'm leaving you all my sewing things as well. Maybe one day you'll meet a nice young lady who can use them. Please keep them safe for me.'

I looked at her and she winked, but I dldn't know why, I was just too dumbfounded. 'Of course, Uncle Rick and Auntie Bess, I'm honoured,' I managed to stammer, overcome with emotion.

That was the last time I saw Uncle Rick alive. He died of a heart attack a few weeks later and Aunt Bess soon followed. I went to both of their funerals and was quite surprised to find Trev at his mother's. I was soon to find out why. The reading of the will took place immediately afterwards. I didn't have much stomach for it until it came to Uncle Rick's apparatus. It was with disbelief that I heard it had been left to Trev. I was too upset to protest, but I knew deep in my heart that Tricky Trev had been up to his old tricks. I got up and headed for the door, trying not to look at smirking Trev, who obviously knew about Uncle Rick's secret stash. I was just about to brush past him when the vicar, who had presided over the funerals, stopped me and drew Trev and me together.

'I'm sorry about your parents and your uncle and aunt.' He spoke to us in turn. 'I know this is probably not the time to raise this, but as your father's given long service to the church with his magical shows and will be sadly missed, I wondered, if as a memorial to him, Trevor, that you'd let Michael put on one last show at the village hall, with your father's things?'

What neither of us knew was that all my uncle's magic stuff had been taken to the village hall, at my uncle's request, the night before he died. I could see Trev's face contorting and twisting, but he was not about to antagonise the vicar. He reluctantly agreed, with the proviso that all of the equipment be taken to his father's cottage immediately afterwards. A small imp inside my head started to foment a plan and the thought of revenge was sweet.

I'll not bore you with the details of the show that night, but I was proud to wear my uncle's costume in memory of him. As I waited to go on stage I donned the red 'fox' gloves and regarded the magic box, on its stand, with a broad smile. The finale was to be my uncle's finale when he entered his own special magical cabinet and vanished from the stage in a puff of smoke. He never did like taking a bow and this saved him the trouble. Only this time, as a slight deviation, I was planning to take his magic case with me.

The magical heist went perfectly, and as the cloud blossomed behind me, to rapturous applause (I'd done my uncle proud), I vanished from the cabinet clutching the case to me, and reappeared as quickly as I could at the back door of the village hall, where my car was parked. As I opened the boot to pop the case in, a hand fell on my shoulder and I turned to see the local bobby with my cousin, Trev.

'Hello, hello, hello,' I said. 'What's all this then, Constable?'

The young constable was not too pleased to have his line stolen, but retorted with one that I could not use. 'Michael Magely, you are under arrest.'

At the small police station I was taken to, the magic case was put on the desk in front of the sergeant. 'I caught him red-handed, Sarge!' the young constable declared.

'He certainly did,' I said, displaying my red gloves.

The lanky constable and the burly sergeant put me in mind of Laurel and Hardy, and the sergeant showed the same long-suffering intolerance of fools.

'Open it up,' he said.

The constable opened the case and regarded the contents.

'No!' said Trev. 'There's a secret compartment, that's where the money is stashed! Tell him to open it.'

I realised then that Trev had no idea how to open the magic case, but then how would he? The sergeant looked at me with a pained expression, I could tell he thought the whole matter just a petty theft, but my heart was beating much louder than it had when I walked out on stage less than an hour before. 'It's all right, Sergeant,' I sighed. 'If you insist. It's a fair cop! Presto Digitator!' I tapped and the panel fell open. There was a loud pop and suddenly a shower of feathers exploded into the air and began to drift slowly down around us. I almost expected the sergeant to say this was another fine mess his constable had got him into. Instead the constable, give him his due, dug deep into the secret compartment for the elusive cash. All he pulled out was a pack of needles, some cotton reels and one of those light bulbs that Aunt Bess would use for her sewing that gave a natural light.

'Look, Sarge,' he said, holding the latter aloft, 'it's an open and shut case of daylight robbery.'

The sergeant didn't laugh, but I was bursting with relief, as well as profound puzzlement. *Magic,* I thought, trying to keep a straight face.

Trev, well known to the locals, was threatened with wasting police time, when a detailed search showed no sign of the missing money, on my person or in my car, and left the village without bothering to pick up his father's case, which I gratefully took home.

So it was that one day as I sat with my uncle's magic case and aunt's sewing case, fondly recalling happy childhood memories of them both, I noticed for the first time a similarity between the two cases. Aunt Bess' sewing case was about the same shape and construction as Uncle Rick's case, although covered with bright, flowery material, with red foxgloves on it, while Uncle Rick's was leather. I put them together and realised that Uncle Rick must have made them both.

'I wonder,' I said out loud, and then taking the wand I tapped the sewing box and declared, 'Presto Digitalis.' The same secret panel popped open and out rolled the hundred dollar bill rolls.

'Thanks Uncle Rick! Thanks Aunt Bess,' I said. 'You are both truly magic.'

Lucy And Her Unusual Pet

C M A Hughes

Lucy woke up feeling refreshed early one Sunday morning. As she lay in her bed she listened to the sound of the summer birds singing. It was a lovely day. Lucy yawned and her mouth stretched wide open. Then she stretched out her short arms and legs and kicked off her white sheet and the Pink Panther blanket from the warmth of her bed.

Lucy was so happy to see another day. She was in such a hurry that she jumped out of bed. Her excitement soon came to a sudden end. Somehow she had tangled her big toe in the pink rug by her bed. Without any warning, Lucy came crashing to the floor with a very loud bang. She was very lucky that she did not bang her head on her pine bed. Lucy lay on the floor for a few seconds and did not move a muscle.

Lucy's mother was very worried. She ran from the kitchen to the bottom of the steep stairs. As she ran she called out, 'Lucy! Lucy! What are you doing?'

'Nothing, Mum!' Lucy replied as she rubbed her forehead.

'Well, whatever was that loud bang?'

'Oh, I tripped over the rug!' Lucy said as she sprang to her feet.

'Are you all right my love?' her mother replied in a much softer voice.

'Yes Mum, I am fine.'

'Be more careful darling,' her mother said as she walked slowly back to the kitchen.

Lucy was a little dizzy and shaky as she walked towards the wicker chair close to the large bedroom windows. Lucy stood on the chair so she could reach the pink flowery curtains. She pulled and pulled at the curtains to drawn them back. Lucy was blinded by the sun that beamed on the windowpanes. She half closed her eyes. There was a clear blue sky and as Lucy looked up high into it, there was just one white fluffy cloud which passed slowly by. Lucy whispered, 'Oh, what a lovely day!'

Lucy could not wait to get dressed ready to go downstairs. She dragged off her nightie and then she tugged on her tight jeans which were hard to button up around her waist. Lucy slipped her shoes on. Then she pulled her floppy T-shirt over her head and down over her body. Now she was ready to go downstairs. Lucy called out to her mother, 'Coming Mum!' as she jumped down every step. She made such a noise from the top to the bottom of the stairs. Lucy banged the lounge door behind her then asked her mother where her hairbrush was.

'On the sofa, love, where you left it last night.'

'Oh! Thanks Mum!' Lucy replied as she skipped towards the downstairs bathroom.

Lucy dragged a black plastic stool towards the washbasin, stepped up on it and picked up her Pink Panther toothbrush and gel. Then she scrubbed her teeth up and down, inside and out. She also used a bit of Mum's mouthwash. Next she splashed some warm water on her face and patted her face dry just like Mum had shown her with her own little pink towel. Then she rushed to the lounge, sat on the sofa and brushed her long, brown, wavy hair. Lucy shouted out to her mother to come and help her. Her mother came into the room, sat next to her and brushed her hair, then tied it back with a pretty pink band. Lucy's thick long hair looked nice hanging down to her waist.

Lucy was about to go out of the back door into the garden when her mother called out to her, 'Where do you think you are going, young lady? What about your breakfast? Then there is Sunday school and we have to go to Aunty Meg's for lunch.'

Breakfast was the last thing Lucy had on her mind as she called out to her mother, 'See you later, Mum, I have to look for Barney!'

'Barney? Who is Barney?' her mother asked.

'He's my pet snail.'

'Whatever do you want a dirty snail called Barney for?'

Lucy snapped back, 'Mum, he is different.'

'Why is he so special?'

'Well, he has a larger, darker brown shell than the other snails.' Lucy sighed and begged, 'I must go and find him, I have not seen him since yesterday morning.'

'Hurry up then, and don't be long.'

Barney seemed to be the most important thing in the world to Lucy at the moment. *Breakfast and everything else can wait until later,* she thought as she ran up the garden path to the rockery. Lucy knelt down at the rockery and began to turn every grey pebble over. She searched in vain for Barney. Then she marched up and down every inch of the garden.

Lucy sighed, there was no sign of Barney. Lucy thought and thought. *Maybe Barney had risked going next door.* Lucy decided to peer through some small holes in Mr Jones' garden fence. So she tiptoed up and down so she could reach every hole and looked from one hole to another into her neighbour's garden. Lucy screamed out,

'Oh no! It looks like my Barney is stuck, he is trapped in the netting on the pond. I must get him out!' she cried. 'Before it is too late!'

Lucy ran to Mr Jones' house and knocked on the front door. No one came so she knocked louder. Still no one answered. Lucy took herself off into her neighbour's garden. Sure enough, there was Barney. He was tangled and lay as limp as could be in the net near the edge of the fishpond.

'Oh Barney!' Lucy whispered as she splashed him with cold water from the fishpond. 'Come on my pet, get better!' she said, and splashed him again with the water until she saw him move. 'Hang on Barney, I won't be long!'

Lucy ran home to fetch a pair of scissors to free Barney. When Lucy returned home, her mother asked her to have breakfast or they would be late for church and Aunty Meg's. Lucy was cross with her mother and snapped back, 'Mum, Barney is stuck, I need a pair of scissors please!'

'Where is he stuck?'

'In Mr Jones' back garden, he is tangled in the net on the fishpond.'

Lucy's mother found a small pair of nail scissors and told Lucy to put them in her pocket. Lucy ran back to Mr Jones' garden. She had to take great care as she snipped the nylon around Barney's neck and tail end. He then dropped lifeless into Lucy's left hand. Next, Lucy splashed him with the cold water again and again, and then Barney slid under his shell. Now Barney was out of sight under his dark brown shell in Lucy's warm hand as she walked slowly home.

Back in her garden, Lucy placed Barney on a lettuce leaf in the vegetable patch and stood back to watch him. Lucy waited and waited, it seemed like ten minutes had passed, then another ten minutes. Suddenly Barney popped out his head, feelers and tail end. Next he started to eat some of the fresh green lettuce leaf. Lucy was so happy that she stood there laughing with relief for Barney, looked the best he could ever be. Lucy was so pleased that she showed Barney to her mother. Her mother told her to take more care of him.

Then Lucy's father returned home and saw Barney in Lucy's hand. Lucy told him all about Barney. Lucy's father went into the garden shed and brought out an old fish tank so that Lucy could keep Barney as a real pet. Lucy was so happy that she laughed and tears ran down her rosy cheeks.

Now the whole family were happy and they could get ready for church and later go to Aunty Meg's for lunch.

A Little Star In The Snow

(Dedicated to Christopher Vandeldt who inspired this story; and to his daughter, Cydnee Zeline Vandeldt, who, it is hoped, will be inspired by it.)

Rosemary Yvonne Vandeldt

There were only two weeks left until the end of the Christmas term and everyone was very busy getting ready for the school concert. Chris could not help being caught up in the general excitement as he helped to paint scenery and take messages from one teacher to another.

'Christopher is such a helpful little boy,' the head teacher told his mother, 'I really can't think what we should do without him!'

Chris was not pleased with this praise. He would rather have had a part - even a small one - in a show, but he was never chosen. He sometimes stuttered, especially when he was nervous or excited, and he knew this was why he always stayed behind the scenes as his friends took a bow in the bright theatrical lights.

Petra, his sister, was different. She could sing and dance, she was very pretty and, as usual, she had a big part to play in her class contribution to the Christmas show.

Their parents were immensely proud of her and had bought many tickets - they were bringing Chris' grandparents, his aunt and uncle, three cousins and even some of the neighbours. Every evening, after supper, his mother busied herself at the sewing machine. Petra was to dance in a ballet called 'Eastern Lights'; she had to sing two songs on her own and take a prominent part in a short Nativity play, so she needed many changes of costume.

The day of the concert arrived and Chris and Petra returned to school after an early tea. Petra had to be there at least an hour before the show was due to start and Chris could guarantee he would be needed. He had already spent the afternoon helping to get the stage ready and putting out rows and rows of chairs for the audience. He would, he knew, probably spend the evening running from class to class with urgent messages and giving out programmes.

'Thank goodness you're early, Christopher,' said Mrs Hogan, his class teacher, 'Mrs O'Leary wants to see you right away. Hurry, will you?'

Mrs O'Leary was the class teacher for the oldest pupils in the school. When Chris arrived she was looking harassed. The old cotton wool 'snowman' needed for the evening's final ballet had disintegrated and she was holding in her hands the limp, rather grubby remnants of the sad, overused creature whilst her pupils stood around her, looking on tragically. Mrs O'Leary looked closely at Chris, then she nodded her head. 'Perfect!' she remarked to another teacher who was helping her to get her pupils ready for the show. 'He's just the right size - he will look better than that old cotton wool model and, anyway, we can't possibly mend it or make another one in the time. Actually, now I think of it, we can do more with a live snowman!'

She took Chris by the arm and led the surprised boy to the hall where the stage was. 'We'd like you to do a big favour for us,' she was saying as they walked.

Chris nodded. He was used to doing favours for people.

'Would you take part in our dance - be the snowman? We shall have to dress you in a sheet and put a scarf round your neck and give you a pipe and a top hat.'

Chris could hardly believe it - he would be on the stage that night after all, and he knew that the dance in question was called 'The Brave Little Snowman' so he would, in fact, have the title role!

'We must practise quickly,' Mrs O'Leary was saying, 'come along - I'll show you what to do.'

There was tremendous excitement as the children chattered and giggled whilst they were dressing. The guests arrived and were shown to their seats by other 'helpful' children who were not taking part in the show.

Chris did not see the concert, although he could hear the audience's enthusiastic applause. He was wrapped in a dazzling white sheet, he wore a black top hat and a brightly coloured scarf was wound around his neck. Theatrical make-up had whitened his face. He was very hot but he spent the waiting time standing perfectly still as he knew he must when he took his place before the audience.

When it was time for the final scene of the concert the stage was quickly made ready with the sparkling white trees and hills Chris had, himself, helped to paint.

He waited in his place behind the curtains at the back of the stage. The girls from the top class wore coats which were deeply coloured and trimmed with fur, and some of them had woolly scarves to show how cold it was supposed to be. The dancers gathered, as rehearsed, at the back of the stage and pretended to be digging. They were all taller than Chris so he could be brought through onto the stage without being seen; then the dancers parted and he stood in the bright lights. He could not see the audience and wondered if his parents knew him under his white make-up. The girls pranced admiringly round him and threw cotton wool 'snowballs' at each other, then they left the stage as the lights dimmed to show that it was nightfall.

Standing alone in the blue-tinged stage light, Chris was showered from above with fluttering 'snowflakes'. Then came the boy performers. They entered wearing masks for they were supposed to be robbers. With exaggeratedly guilty movements they made it plain to the audience that they intended to enter the little house erected at the side of the platform, but Chris, 'The Brave Little Snowman', turned to look at each one of them and, in the semi-darkness, they mimed their fear and left the stage, tumbling over one another in their haste. Once again Chris stood in the bright light as the girls returned to dance proudly around him.

'He's really very good,' said Mrs O'Leary to Chris' own teacher, 'after all, he had very little practice. A lot of older boys could not stand so still!'

The dance had ended and it was time for the performers to take a bow. Chris' place was, of course, in the centre of the stage. The light caught the face of his mother as she sat on the end of one of the front rows. She was looking surprised and extremely proud - yes, just as proud as she always looked when little Petra sang and danced and made people clap loudly!

After the concert there was a surprise party for the children. The parents and teachers together had prepared a festive supper for them - and in the centre of the table there was a big white Christmas cake bearing a little snowman who looked very much as Chris had looked earlier that night!

Chris felt excited and energetic and he excelled in the Christmas games the grown-ups had organised. He hardly stopped talking all night and guess what? He did not stutter once!

Several years have passed since that exciting night. In the time that followed, Chris' speech difficulty lessened until it was, at last, totally absent. He took increasingly important parts in theatrical productions, both in and out of school. He has just completed his course at drama school with the highest marks in his year and seems set to embark on a brilliant career.

Thank you so much, you tatty old cotton wool snowman!

Greed

Reana Beauly

Witch Griselda was in a grumpy mood, even when she had made the pots and pans whirl around the room, made her broomstick dance and her three-legged stool turn somersaults, it hadn't made her feel any better.

'It's that Wizard Orgnoff, he always seems to get everything and he doesn't even seem to try before something lands in his lap,' grumbled Witch Griselda.

Ercon, Witch Griselda's apprentice entered the room. Ercon was learning about magic potions and magic spells by helping Witch Griselda, he asked Witch Griselda what he had to collect from the forest today.

'Nothing,' snapped Witch Griselda, and she had flown Ercon outside before he could even blink an eye.

Oh, it's going to be one of those days, thought Ercon, *well I may as well go and visit my cousin Finkle-Dee who will be going to the fair today, at least she is always happy and smiling.*

With his decision made Ercon set off with a jaunty step towards his cousin's house, smiling to himself at the thoughts of the fun they would have at the fair.

Wizard Orgnoff had had a very busy day, he had had to mediate when the Township of Del's council had met, do a magic show for the children at the town fair and help sort out a dispute over whose gate it was because the two paths that led from the gate went to two different houses. Giving one party the inside of the gate and giving the other party the outside of the gate ended the dispute.

Because Witch Griselda was in such a bad mood all of the flowers had wilted and their colour had faded so, Wizard Orgnoff had to do a magic spell to bring them back to their former glory.

Witch Griselda was even more furious than she had been before, she had needed some herbal plants and toe of newt from the forest after all and she couldn't find her apprentice Ercon anywhere to gather them for her, she had to go into the forest herself to look for them. Everyone who lived in the Township of Del always knew when Witch Griselda was furious, because all the milk turned sour, the bread wouldn't rise and the hens stopped laying their eggs.

Having collected her herbal plants and her toe of newt, Witch Griselda made her way back to her cottage grumbling that it was all the fault of her apprentice Ercon that she had to collect her own ingredients for her magic potions. Of course, it was Witch Griselda's own fault because she had dismissed Ercon when he had offered to gather her ingredients for her.

'If only I could get hold of some of Wizard Orgnoff's magic spells it would make me more powerful, but how would I do it?' A plan slowly started to manifest in Witch Griselda's mind.

Wizard Orgnoff was so tired after his busy day, he decided to have an early supper and go to bed, which he did, taking his book of magic spells with him. The Wizard Orgnoff was sleeping so soundly, he didn't hear the squeak of Witch Griselda's pet bat, Sneakums as it entered his bedroom through a slit in the wall that the turret had for windows. Giving another tiny squeak the bat landed on Wizard Orgnoff's table, but the book of magic spells was nowhere to be seen.

Sneakums, seeing something on the floor, flew down to see what it was. Realising he had discovered one of the Wizard Orgnoff's spells, Sneakums picked it up and carried it back to Witch Griselda. Witch Griselda was delighted. She had given the bat Sneakums the power to see and read with a magic spell, she also gave him some of her own power to prolong the length of the magic spell so it wouldn't wear off before Sneakums had a chance to arrive back at her cottage before he had discovered any of the Wizard Orgnoff's spells.

For twelve consecutive nights Witch Griselda used her magic spell, giving the bat Sneakums a little of her own power also, but what Witch Griselda didn't know was that on the second night Wizard Orgnoff had heard the squeak of the little bat as he had landed on the stone floor and got up to investigate. Recognising Witch Griselda's pet bat Sneakums, Wizard Orgnoff waited to see what the bat would do, saw him go to his stand, where he usually kept his magic book of spells and pick up the loose page that Wizard Orgnoff had been working on and carried it out of the tower.

Ah, thought Wizard Orgnoff, s*o that's what Witch Griselda is up to, combining the two lots of spells to give her more power.* A plan started to form in Wizard Orgnoff's mind.

There, thought Witch Griselda, *twelve of Wizard Orgnoff's magic spells should be enough,* and she started to memorise them.

It was mid morning and Witch Griselda again couldn't find her apprentice Ercon anywhere, so she had gone into the woods to find her eye of toad, herbs and sap from the willow tree. As Witch Griselda gathered her ingredients she espied Wizard Orgnoff resting under a chestnut tree. Witch Griselda thought, *Now is my chance to prove to Wizard Orgnoff that I am more powerful than he is.*

Fastening the lid of the jar that her ingredients were in, Witch Griselda stealthily crept up to Wizard Orgnoff. Firing a bolt of lightning, her own spell as well as Wizard Orgnoff's spell, she couldn't wait to see the result, but nothing happened.

Wizard Orgnoff rose from his resting place under the chestnut tree and turned to face Witch Griselda. Witch Griselda realised she had been discovered. Throwing balls of fire, more lightning and as many magic spells as she could remember, Witch Griselda was astounded to find nothing worked.

'So, Witch Griselda, it wasn't enough that you terrified all of the inhabitants of the Township of Del, you wanted to have my magic spells as well as your own, to make you more powerful so you could be stronger than I am. What you didn't know, Witch Griselda, was that I had espied your pet bat Sneakums on the second night he came and realised you had placed a magic spell upon him giving him the power to read my spells, so each night I left out on my stand discarded spells, useless ones, for him to find.'

Quaking, Witch Griselda realised that Wizard Orgnoff had beaten her, but couldn't understand why some of her own magic spells hadn't worked, then suddenly it came to her what had happened. In her haste to gain some of Wizard Orgnoff's spells she hadn't realised every time she was giving Sneakums some of her own power to strengthen the magic spell her own power was diminishing. 'I gave away my power,' said Witch Griselda, very annoyed at herself.

'For your greed to gain more power you will be turned into a tree and stand in the forest forever,' said Wizard Orgnoff. On saying this, he turned Witch Griselda into an old gnarled tree and to this day the people of the Township of Del still tell the story of Witch Griselda, her greed and how she lost her power.

So remember never to give away your power to other people.

The Rainbow's End

Bryony Freeman

At the bottom of her garden, the oak tree stands, its branches reaching out to the distant lands. So climb me smart adventurous children, I'll take you to another land, where the colours are forever and a child's fortune can be in your hands.

So the children climb the mighty tree, searching for the rainbow's door, it shines to show them the way, the prizes that will be in store. The winding road, a mile long, the journey they must take, it has pretty views and nasty little men standing at the gates. Their long sharp nails and beady eyes, sharp pink tongues and mighty cries.

The mighty sun shining bright illuminates the land, they must beware of the evil monsters holding out their hands.

There are two signs, 'Pot of Gold End', 'The Monster's Village', beware children, the route you take, treasures may guide your way or little beings will lead your dainty bodies the wrong way.

The children pick the Pot of Gold and walk along the pretty road, avoiding caves and shadowed faces. The black well of the dark and cold and witches cooking plump little toads, and big branched trees with nasty faces pointing towards nasty places, running for miles against the sudden storms and craters in the ground, which swallow up little children like helpless worms without a sound, into a world where you cannot escape. It is a world where you can only wait for a black unicorn to fly you back to better lands, the old moon, the whispers in the heavy sands.

Suddenly they see the light which would win against the blackest night, the treasure chest of great delight of merry games and precious times. In the chest the pot of gold, welcoming the children home. Make your wish, take one gift, share my treasures for other's dreams. Then when you do I will wish you home safe and sound, where I swear good children you will never be alone.

A Summer's Day In Derrybeg

Ellen Spiring

The two young Irish girls, Biddy and Mary, were enjoying an idyllic summer's day walking by the river picking buttercups and daisies for making daisy chains and crowns and sitting down by the river in the hot sunshine dangling their feet in the cool water. The cloudless sky was an azure blue, everywhere was lush with numerous shades of green. The two friends had decided to eat their lunch of soda bread and bacon, Mammy's caraway seed cake, all washed down with ginger beer.

'Ah, shor, it's a lovely day Biddy, I don't want the summer to end, the winters are so cold and damp in Derrybeg,' Mary sighed and laid back on the riverbank contentedly.

Biddy did likewise and they spent one hour 'taking the sun' when suddenly Biddy jumped to her feet with an excited look upon her face. ' Mary, me ma and da are going out tonight to The Harp and Lyre. There's a caeliegh on and they'll be 'three sheets to the wind' and late home, why don't you come over to my house, and we'll walk down to the boreen to see if we can spot any of the 'little people'. There's a fairy ring down there and if we wait quietly we may catch a sight of them, we might even get a crock of gold left by the king of the leprechauns. If we take me da's box camera with us we might get a picture. Shall we go Mary?'

Mary agreed to go over early evening. 'The evening should be light enough, if the leprechauns do come to dance around the fairy ring Liam Leprechaun will play his fiddle, they'll be in their best greens, buckles and hornpipe shoes. Ah, shor it would be a sight to behold and if the king is there and leaves a crock of gold, we'd be rich to the end of our days. Biddy, think of all the summers. God almighty, we could go to all the sunny places, summer all the time. Bliss, sheer bliss, be the jaysus.'

The girls laid back and dreamed on, their imagination running riot. Early that evening Biddy's ma and da took themselves off to The Harp and Lyre. Before they went Biddy asked if it was all right for Mary to call.

'As long as you don't get into any mischief and be back while it's still light, take a jacket with you in case it gets cooler,' instructed her mammy. With that they went out.

Mary waited until her parents got their glad rags on and got similar instructions from her mammy, then she set out to meet Biddy to look for the little people at the end of the boreen, the beautiful leafy glade at the end of the country lane, particularly lovely in the summertime with the perfume of wild flowers pervading the air and birds' song echoing through the woods.

Mary walked along as if in a dream, she loved nature and marvelled at the small creatures that came out of hiding places as if to greet her. Mary listened for sounds of laughter and music, especially a fiddle. She thought to herself how two years previously she thought she had seen the leprechaun she had named Liam with his fiddle, on such a summer's evening.

The sky was changing colour from blue to pink as the sun was beginning to set. Biddy was waiting in the lane. 'Come on you slow coach or the light will be gone, I had such a search for me da's camera.'

They crept quietly to their watching place, the air was warm, the evening tranquil. The girls settled themselves and looked and listened hard at the fairy ring, willing the fairy folk to come out to dance.

Biddy broke the silence and whispered to Mary, 'Do you think they will come? I'm getting a numb backside sitting here. Did you bring any sweets? I could do to suck something.'

'I've some humbugs in me bag, Biddy, but don't eat them all. Didn't you have your tea about an hour ago.'

'Indeed I did but me ma only gave me salad and soda bread, it never fills me up for long, pratees are best.'

'Ah shor, that's why you're the size you are,' complained Mary as Biddy put two more humbugs into her mouth, 'save one or two for me greedy.'

Suddenly there was a hush and the sound of music, a jig, yes, definitely a jig, played by a fiddle. They looked toward the ring, then there was a rustling in the big oak tree, Biddy took out the camera and set it up to take a picture. Mary chattered excitedly.

'Will you shut up you eejit, I'm trying to see and listen, I suggest you do the same.'

'Diddle dum, diddle dum, diddle I dum dum
Into the fairy ring I come.
I have the fiddle, now get off your bum,
Diddle I, Diddle I, diddle I dum dum.
You can dance, you can prance, you can sing a song,
I will play you a jig then you can't be wrong.'

More of the leprechauns appeared as if from nowhere. They danced around the tree and the fairy ring. A jig then a reel. What a colourful sight, all in green and gold with silver buckles on hats, belts and shoes, flashing when the light caught them. Most of the elders had whiskers and beards and pointed ears, gnome-like in appearance.

The two friends clung to one another in excitement.

'Take some pictures Biddy, quick, quick,' Mary urged her friend on.

'Jaysus I'm doing my best to focus on them, stop tugging at my arm. Mary, let go!'

Click and click went the camera.

'Is the king there, can you see him with me crock of gold?'

'Be patient you omathaun, if they hear you they'll go and the king won't come with 'our' crock of gold,' snapped Biddy.

She was a born bossy boots that one was. Following a few more clicks of the camera, jigs and reels later the fairy folk sat down to rest and eat, yes, bacon and soda bread.

By that time the sun had gone a vibrant red and out from a hole in the tree came the king. He was dressed the same but his buckles were gold and he wore a crown instead of a hat, in his hands was the crock.

'God almighty would you look at him, ah shor, the light is going, everything will be red on the film, if it comes out at all.'

'Take one anyway, you never know, think of the summers we can have if he leaves the crock behind.'

Biddy did as she was told, click, when . . . suddenly the leprechauns left as quickly as they came. A silence hung over the boreen. Mary and Biddy cautiously walked to the ring and there in the middle of it was the crock of gold coins.

'You see they did come, they do exist Biddy.'

The girls took up the pot and ran home. They didn't sleep that night. The next day Biddy took the film to the chemist and gushed out the story, except for the crock of gold.

'It will be a week, call in a week,' he said.

'A week? said Biddy, impatient to see the results. The week came and went, the girls went back together to Derrybeg.

'It's a shame,' said the chemist, 'but you have some lovely scenery. Not a leprechaun in sight on the photographs though, you must have imagined it.'

The two friends knew different, they had seen and heard and the crock and its contents were hidden away in Biddy's secret place. Oh yes, there would be more summer days in Ireland but when they were older there would be the summers abroad all thanks to the leprechaun king and Liam and the fairy folk, not on the pictures but they do exist insisted Mary. Imagination indeed.

The Three Elephants

A Hardy

In a land not far away from here lived three elephants, Mummy Elephant, Daddy Elephant and Baby Elephant.

They lived in a pretty little cottage in the countryside. The cottage was next to a beautiful wood and in the spring, when the weather was becoming warmer and the birds were beginning to sing, they would go for walks through the wood. They would walk slowly and lazily, gazing at the beauty around them. Baby Elephant would always follow his mother and father, curling his trunk around the tail in front of him, so that he wouldn't get lost.

When they got to the middle of the wood, they always stopped, because, in the middle of the wood, there were the most beautiful flowers you could hope to see. There were so many beautiful flowers stretching away into the distance, and, as Baby Elephant stood there, he would smell the flowers - it was the sweetest smell you could imagine, and he would be lost in his dreams. After a while they would take a last look at the flowers on their left, and then slowly turn to the right and retrace their steps home, careful that their big feet didn't trample on any of the flowers.

This day was even hotter than normal when Mummy and Baby Elephant decided to take their walk. As they trundled slowly off, they raised their heads to say goodbye to Daddy Elephant who wanted to stay at home to finish his work. He was painting the outside of their cottage, a big, big paintbrush held in his trunk. His trunk already had splashes of pink paint all over it.

Holding his mother's tail as she ambled slowly off through the trees, Baby Elephant followed, looking round, as he always did, at the beautiful countryside around him.

Eventually they got to the middle of the wood. Baby Elephant stared at the mass of flowers before him, and the rainbow of colours: orange, red, yellow and blue. But his favourites were the purple flowers.

Because it had been such a lovely morning, they had left a little earlier on their trip than normally, and suddenly his mother had an idea. 'Let's not go straight back home,' she said, 'let's spend a little time walking amongst the flowers for a change.'

Baby Elephant was thrilled and, his trunk holding excitedly to his mother's tail, he waited for her to turn left into the flowers. As he did so, he breathed in deeply, and for a moment the beautiful scent of the flowers made him dizzy with joy.

Then he looked down to follow his mother, but she wasn't there! She had disappeared! He looked up at the flowers, but he still couldn't see her. He became suddenly very scared and called out her name, but there was no answer, just the sound of his nervous cry dying out in the distance. He looked to the right where the trees were quite thick and realised his mother must have changed her mind and decided to go home, thinking he would automatically follow.

He decided to go home to make sure. Still very worried, he quickly walked through the wood, his big body swaying from side to side in his haste.

When he got to the cottage he could see a lot more pink paint on the walls and on his father's trunk, but no sign of his mother.

'Hello. Back already? Where's your mother?'

'Isn't she here?' he blurted out, almost unable to speak.

His father looked at him sharply.

'What's happened?' he asked.

When Baby Elephant had breathlessly explained everything, his father quickly decided what to do. 'Take me back to where you last saw her. We'll find her. She's just got lost, that's all. Hold tight to my tail.'

Tossing his paintbrush aside, his father moved firmly off, and Baby Elephant followed, trying to keep up with his father's steps, sometimes bumping into him as he ran after him. Breathing hard, he guided his father so that they exactly traced the steps followed earlier by himself and his mother.

When they got to the middle of the wood, he told his father to stop by the flowers.

'What happened next?' his father asked.

'She turned left into the flowers, instead of turning right to the cottage.'

'OK,' his father said slowly and calmly, 'we'll do the same. Then we'll find her.'

Baby Elephant had such confidence in his father that he no longer felt worried, and knew everything would be all right. He turned to look at the flowers, and once again all the yellows and blues and purples, and their magic smell, seemed to invade his mind and body and put him in a trance, just for a moment.

Shaking his head, like shaking off sleep, he looked down to follow his father, but to his horror, his father wasn't there! He had disappeared! Baby Elephant's heart missed a beat and he wanted to cry. He looked quickly to see if his father was walking among the flowers, but he couldn't see anybody.

'Daddy! Daddy!' he called out, but a stony silence answered him. He tried to call out again, but he was so scared the words wouldn't come out of his mouth.

He almost panicked, and would have begun to run here and there without any purpose, and got lost, if he hadn't suddenly remembered his parents' advice. They had told him never to lose his head if something went wrong, and always go home if he were separated from them and found himself alone. Perhaps his father had seen his mother in the wood, and had gone off in that direction. Yes, he was sure that was it. They were probably both in the cottage now.

Baby Elephant quickly walked through the wood, sure he would find them, but the rustling sound of his feet on the grass and twigs made him feel strangely alone.

As he approached the cottage he could see its walls half-painted in pink, and the paintbrush on the ground where his father had dropped it, but nothing else. He didn't have the courage to call out, but, once inside the cottage, he looked into each room. They were all empty. He burst into tears. He was on his own, and he was scared!

Trying to be a big elephant, he wiped the tears from his eyes with his trunk, and thought and thought. What must he do? What would his father do?

Then he realised there was only one thing he could do. He would have to return to the middle of the wood where the flowers were. If his parents weren't at home, then they had to be somewhere in the wood.

He slowly retraced his steps, for, try as he might to walk fast, his legs felt wobbly and weak. How he wished he had a tail in front of him to keep hold of and guide him safely along the way!

When he got back to the flowers, he stopped and listened. There was an absolute silence. There was nobody to be seen. What could he do?

He realised he had to go where his father and mother had gone. He had to turn left into the flowers. As he turned left, he nervously looked at the flowers and once more caught a whiff of their sweetness. Then, stirring himself again, he looked down at the ground before him. His heart missed a beat. He couldn't see his feet! He looked at where his trunk should have been, but there was nothing there! He had disappeared!

He was frantic! Unable to think, he found himself retracing the path back to the cottage. When he got near, he looked up. But he wasn't there! There was nobody there, neither outside nor inside.

His heart beating louder and louder, he found himself rushing off once again through the wood. What could he do but forever retrace and retrace his steps?

He arrived at the flowers again, totally puzzled. There was only silence and emptiness. And then it came to him! He must turn right and return to the cottage. He mustn't turn left into the flowers! It was so simple.

As soon as he turned right he could see his big feet stepping out ahead of him and his trunk swaying before his eyes. He was back again!

Elated, he rushed through the wood, no longer worried. As he approached the beautiful cottage he looked up. His mother and father were standing outside and contemplating the totally pink walls with satisfaction, his father holding the paintbrush in his totally pink trunk. They turned round as they heard him coming, and he rushed towards them, his eyes brimming with tears of joy.

'Here he is,' said his mother. 'We knew you would work out what to do in the end. You found out that you must never turn left into the flowers. When you do that, you disappear. They are magic flowers. If you turn right, everything is all right. We've been waiting for you. You've been a very clever elephant. Now, let's go inside and have lunch.'

Daisy Duckling

A R Carter

Daisy was a very happy duckling. She lived in a big pond with her mummy and daddy and her brothers and sisters. She had lots of friends to play with too and her days were very busy. Daisy was only a small duckling and still needed little sleeps during the daytime, so, when she got tired from playing with all her friends, she would find her mummy, snuggle up close to her lovely warm feathers and fall fast asleep.

The pond where Daisy and her family lived was surrounded by trees and shrubs and beneath the trees grew wild flowers amongst the grass. It was lovely in the springtime with all the bluebells and primroses. Daisy would sometimes leave the pond and waddle about under the trees smelling the flowers and feeling the grass tickle her webbed feet. She was careful not to go too far and always made sure she could still see the pond and her friends. She knew it was dangerous to wander away from her mummy and daddy.

Ladies and gentlemen and children would come to the pond with bags of food for all the birds and what a flurry of excitement *that* always caused. Every duck on the pond would rush to the bank where the people were standing, trying to be first in the queue. They weren't very gentle either and Daisy had had one or two pecks from the bigger ducks who were greedy but, on the whole, Daisy liked it when the people came - she liked to watch them throwing the food to all the birds. She would keep her eye on odd bits that fell in quieter waters and then paddle over to eat them in peace.

There was one lady whom Daisy particularly liked and she would watch for her to come walking quietly down the path that led to the pond. This special lady would feed *all* the ducks, but she always made sure that some of the pieces of food landed very near to Daisy because she had noticed how Daisy stayed back when the others were all scrabbling about. The lady would stand and watch Daisy gobbling up the bits of bread and cake and she would smile and nod to herself in a pleased sort of way.

Daisy was growing quickly and her feathers were changing from soft, fluffy, downy ones to larger, stronger ones. She was a mallard duck and when she was fully grown would be brown like her mummy - not all different bright colours like her daddy, a drake mallard. She longed to be grown up and to look like her mummy. When Mummy sailed across the pond she looked really proud and majestic. One day, Daisy would have ducklings of her own and would look after them, keep them warm and show them what to do.

So the days passed. Daisy *still* went up the bank and under the trees to see and smell the wild flowers and let the grass tickle her webbed feet. In the summertime the flowers were different from the springtime ones. There were wood anemones, tiny purple violets and some little blue flowers which were nicknamed 'bird's-eyes'. The lady whom Daisy particularly liked *still* came to the pond and especially looked out for Daisy at the back of the crowd - making sure she got plenty to eat. All the young ducklings *still* played together and just now and again Daisy *still* snuggled up close to her mummy for a little sleep. Yes, Daisy was a very happy duckling.

A Narrow Squeak

Avis E Wolfenden

Albert and Annie were two little mice who lived in a very snug apartment, No 6 Skirting Board Terrace, in a house belonging to a Mr and Mrs Hughes. The Hughes were a nice family with two children and Albert and Annie enjoyed sharing their house, Albert was a smart black mouse who wore a red spotted bow tie. He had long whiskers which twitched whenever there was danger. Annie, his wife, was a pretty grey mouse. They lived quite modestly, going to town once a week on market day. They always managed to save a little money for a rainy day.

Every night when the Hughes family had gone to bed Albert and Annie would peep out of their front door and, if all was clear, out they would come. Having relatives living close by, they all gathered together on the pantry floor for a midnight feast, laughing and talking and catching up on the latest news.

Annie's uncle always brought his fiddle, so they had dancing and played games. The younger mice liked to play 'Oranges and Lemons' and screamed in pretend fright when it came to 'Chop, chop, chop off the last man's head'. Another favourite game was hide-and-seek because where mice live there are always lots of passages and so they had great fun trying to find one another.

Sometimes if the Hughes children had forgotten to put away their toys a lovely time was had by the boy mice who would jump into the toy cars, put on their peaked caps and charge along the lounge carpet pretending they were Grand Prix drivers. Grandad mouse would drop his handkerchief as though it was the chequered finishing flag and there was much bumping, jostling and squeaking as a great time was had by all.

In the meantime the little girl mice gathered up loose silk threads dropped by Mrs Hughes from her embroidery and used them as skipping ropes.

The mummy mice, sitting close by, would knit other pieces of silk into garments for the baby mice. An empty matchbox was a great find and would be quickly made into a cot by a daddy mouse.

One particular night they were all making such a noise and enjoying themselves so much that they didn't notice morning had arrived and they were nearly caught by Mr Hughes, who went to work very early as he was the local milkman. Everyone scurried down the nearest mousehole puffing and panting.

'That was a close shave,' said Albert, 'I thought he had seen us that time.'

When they had recovered from their fright Annie decided she was hungry. 'I could just eat a nice piece of cheese,' she said.

'I'll see what I can find,' said Albert disappearing into the kitchen.

Now unknown to the little mice as Mr Hughes went through the front door, Tom the cat from next door shot into the house and hid behind a chair. The minute that Albert arrived in the kitchen the cat pounced on him, holding under his paw. As everyone knows, mice don't like cats and poor Albert was terrified. 'Help, help!' he squeaked.

Tom laughed. *A tasty morsel,* he thought. *I will keep you for later.*

Annie became more and more worried when Albert did not return and eventually she decided to go and look for him herself. Going quickly but silently into the kitchen she was stopped in her tracks by the sight of Albert held prisoner under Tom's huge paw. She immediately started screaming for help.

The grown-up mice decided that the only thing to do was to rush at the cat. When Tom saw all the mice charging towards him, he was so surprised and frightened, his hair stood on end and, howling, he backed away giving Albert his chance to escape and run with the other mice as fast as he could to the safety of his house.

'Phew, that was a narrow squeak,' he said, straightening his bow tie. 'I've had enough excitement for one day.'

'Not quite,' said Annie, 'I have another surprise.' There in a little matchbox cot were two of the sweetest baby mice he had ever seen; one was black with a little spotted bow tie and one was a pretty little grey mouse. When the babies had been fed and tucked up in their cot, Albert and Annie crept into their bed and were soon fast asleep.

Castle Of The Night

Glenwyn Peter Evans

I always enjoyed my weekend camping trips, with my best friend, Hale; but then one night, a mysterious damp mist encircled our small camp.

'Tuck's! Tuck's!' he yelled, hysterically, 'get out 'ere quick.'

Startled, I bolted upright, snatched the zipper on my sleeping bag, and howled like a baying hound at a full, waxing moon. 'My finger! It's gushing blood!'

Hale, shot through the tent door, 'You've gone through the jugular vein,' he exclaimed excitedly, 'Tucker, yer gonna die!' An expression of genuine horror swept his face.

'Mummy!' I whimpered, pathetically. Hale grunted, throwing me the first aid kit. Still whimpering, finger throbbing madly, I dabbed away, trying to stem the constant blood flow. 'Hale's, how long have I got? Shouldn't we use a tourniquet?'

Hale frowned thoughtfully, 'Come with me,' he gestured.

Shakily, I staggered to my feet, nursing my throbbing, poorly finger.

'We have a serious problem,' rasping in the cold night air.

Suddenly, a heavy thudding noise wafted the air above us, and as we looked up, two huge talons skimmed our heads; the fluorescent object, screeching horribly, soared, circled, then dived straight for us ...

'Vampire!' screamed Hale, 'he's smelled yer blood!' sprawling the ground.

'It's a barn owl!' managing a quick, nervous laugh. 'Barn owls screech like that, and sometimes give off an eerie glow, scaring the pants off even the bravest of men.'

'I knew that,' snorted Hale, wiping away the damp mud.

'Wow,' I said, pointing. For a minute or so, I forgot my dilemma. 'Its caught a field mouse ...'

'Disgusting,' declared Hale. 'Nasty beast!' The creature tore up its prey; the gore, stringing its bloody beaks. Hale, puked.

The blood would not stop flowing, and by now, I started to panic. 'My finger, Hale,' I pleaded, worriedly. 'Get a doctor, please. It's my jugular vein ...'

'Huh, just remembered,' came a sharp cackle from Hale. 'The jugular vein's in yer neck, cretin.'

I growled, and was all set to go for him, when the air was rent by ear-splitting screeches. Hale looked at me, frighteningly, and jumped straight into my arms, screaming; the bush in front of us shook violently; within split seconds an immense dark creature, scudded the air, with great agility and precision, its cut-throat razor claws, lashing, slashing savagely, it plummeted towards its target.

Hale squealed, I sobbed, the owl, to the beating of its mighty wings, took off, the cat, its matted fur all on end, missed its prey, hit a tree and slumped to the ground, its fangs shredding the bark.

'It's a wildcat,' I exclaimed, nervously. 'And - and it's knocked itself out!'

'Then explain that rasping, horrid screech,' demanded Hale; I dropped him.

'The kettle! You left it on,' I snarled angrily. 'You know Hale, this is a right-fright-night fiasco! And this,' holding aloft the bandaged finger, 'would never have 'appened if you hadn't panicked me ... what was so flamin' important?'

'Important?' screeched Hale, in a squeaky, embittered tone, 'I'll tell yer what's flamin' important, mate; yer forgot to bring the milk and I 'ate tea without milk ... so yer can go and get some.'

'This time of the night? Yer gotta be kiddin'?'

Hale shook his head, sombrely.

'Where from?'

Hale was silent, his stare vacant, his white freckled face, spread like glazed-over semolina pudding, was intensely drawn, while his eyes rolled like shiny marbles, suddenly they flashed black, he bared his teeth and, with a savage, wild-like grimace that scared the ruddy wits out of me, pointed ...

'That castle ... over there,' he said, with a booming, hollow voice.

'What castle, where? I didn't see no ...' My sentence was cut short by a terrible thunderclap, a sheet of white lightning and a spasm of fear that rattled my every nerve.

There, sprawled out through the vapour-like mist, stood the dark, foreboding, gloomy, silhouetted form of a bat-shaped castle. A loathsome thing, sinister-like in all its horrid, gothic appearance, and all I could do was stand, and gasp in awe.

'Spooked?' tittered Hale, horribly.

I gulped back the bile in my throat, 'No,' squeaked I, with pathetic bravado, and devil-don't-care attitude.

'Then yer won't mind ...' voice, trailing, deliberately, slow-like and faint.

'Mind?' I stammered; the ground, unwittingly, moved steadily beneath my feet and before I knew it, unwillingly, I was before a great solid, oak door and, as my index finger hummed and throbbed and oozed with blood, I could not help but notice the uncanny welcome mat with the words 'Welcome', spelt in sweet, sickly, dripping fresh blood, *my blood!*

I screeched in terror. Hale, disappeared, the doors blasted open, lightning hit my butt, and, with a smoking, singeing shriek, I leapt beyond its dripping wet, gaping mouth, into its deep, musty bowels and faced the black dread of nothingness. Quickly, I got up, spun on my heels, and went to walk, nay, run away, but as the door slammed, I came to have this inkling of a whimpering feeling, that I was trapped, and, not alone ...

Alone, in the dark, and very, very much afraid, I whimpered pathetically, and held aloft my hands, groping the mass black pool of instant emptiness. I stood, a lifeless statue, frozen in time, just listening; listening to every wild thumping beat that my heart made.

A faint rumble, then, a clattering roar, it grew in volume and intensity, I gulped, I could hear it scampering, my heart ready to tear apart ... *wait a mo', that ain't me heart* ... no! that was something ... else!

Fear gripped my soul like the cold and icy claw of terror that gripped my right shoulder. I screamed! It screamed! I cried tears! It laughed tears! 'Go away!' I shrieked, only to have it screeched back ...

'It's my voice,' I exclaimed, joyously, as it reverberated and boomed the vast black void. I laughed ... it laughed ... but ... I'd stopped! Now, I was really scared 'Who's there?'

Growling angrily, with an air of deep foreboding and dread, the voice slammed round the room, then, 'Aaaargh,' followed by a dying thud.

'Oooh,' I whined. 'If only I had a torch.'

''Ere, usesh mine ...'

'Why thank you,' I said to the two floating, glaring, staring red eyes.

I shrieked! It gurgled! My hair stood on end! I fumbled the switch, and sighed relief as the beam cut through the dark gloom, danced the room, and the phantom menace vanished.

'What next?' I asked myself, gasping nervously.

'Follow the arrows,' boomed back a hollow, husky voice.

'Arrows?' I rubbed my eyes in disbelief. Nine red arrows came flaring from out of the bleak, black yonder. With an awesome roar, up and up they went, then, disappeared.

All at once, my ears were flicked. 'Ouch,' that hurt. Scanning the room, 'Hey! why's the floor moving? No! Stumbling? Shuffling?

Thrashing even?' Great throngs of ... flesh eating bugs swarmed and squeaked madly, shrilly.

'*Eek!*' I yelled. Waving my torch round, frantically, I began to run, deeper and deeper into the black abyss, only to be stopped, suddenly, by sheer terror, a huge snake seemed to be dropping its coils, slowly, to the floor, and as I traced its source with the beam of my light, I could see, quite clearly, that it came from nowhere and hung on nothingness.

Its loathsome diamond chained head reared and jingled, as if it had chimes attached to its body and for a minute, paralysed me into a lifeless numbness, until the bugs chewed my very feet ...

'A spiral staircase! It's a spiral staircase!' I could have laughed and danced, but the bugs wanted to eat my flesh, I could imagine what their silly little shrilly squeaks were saying to each other: 'Pass me the salt ...' 'What's for desert ...?' 'Mushy brains and bloodied eyeballs ...' I felt mortified, but then, I had an epiphany ... I counted the rungs. Thirty-nine steps. The spiral staircase had thirty-nine steps! And maybe, a way out?

In one bounding, crunching leap, I assailed the air, and landed safely upon the first rung of the spiral staircase. The little rascals squealed, hungrily:

'Wow, dinner's gone off!'

'That's fast food?'

''E's squished Fred!'

'Let's eat Fred ...'

The spiral staircase seemed to hang, uncannily, suspended in mid-air, so I scanned the torch's beam as far as it would go, through the falling, silver dust, beyond the festooned cobwebs too, the biggest, blackest spider I had ever seen!

My stomach knotted, my heart froze and my eyes bulged as boldly I faced the spider from Mars.

Slowly, inquisitively, it came like a creeping shadow, touching each span of the web with its giant feelers, cautiously shaking it gently, in case its prey should escape its inevitable fate; but I was bound by fear, fast and useless.

My body shook, the spiral staircase jingled like wind chimes, the spider rose its head, saliva dripped from its mouth as it slobbered uncontrollably and I fretted that, with every bead of sweat that fell from my shaking, clammy body, it tasted my fear. With a maddening dash, it pounced, I shrieked, its fangs bore down, biting hard! I dropped the torch and the spider fell off, I felt like a darned idiot!

'Good job no one was here, or they'd cry with laughter ...'

Great bellows of laughter boomed the air, the staircase rattled and shook rhythmically, jingling and chiming, simultaneously, my ears were pricked, violently.

'Gerroff!' I cried. *'Stop it!'* screaming frantically to waves of hysterical high-pitched shrieks, squeals, scuffling and flapping.

My torch had broken, I was a prisoner to darkness. 'Oh,' I cried, 'my torch - my torch ...' Somebody handed it back ...

'A repair bill? 'Two new batteries. One new bulb. Brand new, only: £15.00'. What!' I cried. 'Ludicrous! Nightlife robbery! It only costs a pound at Quids-are-in-Land!' But from the dark of night, in he beam of my light, danced the black terror of instant death, a bat out of Hell, its luminous fangs glistening, it swooped for the kill! I weaved, ducked and dived. The wretched creature dropped a dollop on my head then skittered away.

'Pooh!' I yelled, 'I thought only pigeons did that!' shaking my fist in anger! Now I was seething. Enough was enough! Up and up I clambered, round and round. A door! An exit! Around it, radiated spears of light; *zap-zap-zing-zoom;* ricocheting the spiral staircase, one zipped my head, parting my hair; it knocked me back a rung, bumping smack bang into something nasty, smelly and bloody, horrid.

A huge horned wraith with two glaring, yellow eyes, a hairy mush and fantastic, gigantic, trailing eye teeth!

Its hot, stinking breath rippled my face. 'Yummy! Yummy!' it howled.

'Me'seat yer ...' I screamed, pounding the metal staircase, puffing and panting thirstily. It dived for my feet, clawing me back, laughing, reeling me in like a fish on a hook.

I fought as hard as I could, kicking and fisting the air, my punches going nowhere, it screamed, delighted at his tucker. I screamed, not wanting to be his tucker! His talon-like claws tore deep into the flesh of my leg, splattering blood everywhere. His bottom jowl dropped and my legs were within its jaws; I lashed and bashed him, frantically; finally, triumphantly, *wham!* I knocked out his tooth.

'Tucker!' it howled angrily. 'Tucker! wake up, you've clobbered me tooth out!'

'Hale?' I stammered. I was dreaming and covered in his blood ...

Hale's father drove us home, and as Hale was explaining how he lost his tooth, a cold shiver ran up my spine, hovering above us I saw something that made my face whiten and my flesh crawl. A giant bat ... 'Hale,' I whispered feebly, as my poorly finger, throbbed. 'It's here ... the castle of the night ... it wants you ...'

The Wish Fairy

Susan Mary Robertson

Three children lived in a cottage in a village in the countryside. Harry was six years old. He had been going to the school in the village for a year already. Tracey was four years old. She would go to school next year. Charlie was three years old. He was due to go to school in another two years' time when he reached his fifth birthday.

Their father worked on a farm just outside the village. Their mother stayed at home to look after them, the cottage and to make clothes. On fine sunny days the three children went outside to play in the garden. Sometimes they went for a walk with their mother into the village or out into the fields, meadows and woods outside the village. On Saturdays they all went by bus to the nearest town, which was ten miles away, to do their shopping.

One afternoon, Harry, Tracey and Charlie were playing in the back garden behind their cottage. They were playing hide-and-seek around the apple trees, cherry trees, blackberry bushes and rose bushes. Then they wondered what to play next.

Tracey said, 'I wish I was a fairy. Why don't we play fairies and elves?'

Harry laughed. He said, 'You can be a fairy, Charlie can be an elf, but I'm going to be a giant!'

Charlie said, 'It isn't fair that I am so little!' and he started to cry.

Suddenly they saw a sparkle and a puff of blue smoke and heard a tinkling sound. Next, a beautiful blonde fairy wearing a blue dress and carrying a magic wand appeared.

The fairy said, 'I am your Wish Fairy. I can grant you three wishes, one wish each, but you can share each wish together, the oldest one first. What is your wish, Harry?'

Harry thought for about five seconds, and then he said, 'I wish I was an astronaut and we can go to the moon!'

The Wish Fairy waved her magic wand. A spaceship appeared on the lawn next to the rose bushes. Harry, Tracey, Charlie and the Wish Fairy were all dressed in spacesuits.

The Wish Fairy said, 'I would love to go to the moon too, so I shall come with you!'

The Wish Fairy and the three children climbed into the spaceship. Harry and the Wish Fairy then flew it up into space to the moon. They had a safe landing on the moon's rocky and dusty surface, in one of its craters.

They climbed out of the spaceship and had a walk on the moon. They went for a ride in a space buggy. They took photographs of the moon, and also of the Earth, sun and stars, which they could see from the moon.

Then they climbed back into the spaceship and flew back to their cottage garden on Earth.

The Wish Fairy then asked, 'What is your wish, Tracey?'

Tracey said, 'I wish I was a ballerina!'

The Wish Fairy waved her magic wand. Suddenly Tracey and the Wish Fairy were both dressed in white tutus, Harry and Charlie were dressed in black tights, and they all wore ballet shoes. They were standing in the wings of the stage of the ballet at Covent Garden in London.

The conductor waved his baton, the orchestra began to play 'Swan Lake' by Tchaikovsky and the ballet dancers all began to dance. Tracey and the Wish Fairy danced as swans and the two boys danced as two huntsmen. The audience clapped at the end of the ballet. Then the four of them flew back to the garden.

The Wish Fairy then asked, 'What is your wish, Charlie?'

Charlie said, 'I want to be in a circus!'

The Wish Fairy waved her magic wand a third time, and they were all dressed as acrobats in a big circus. Firstly the clowns came in to perform, then an elephant, then a lion tamer and his pride of lions, and then a troupe of monkeys and chimpanzees. The acrobats came on last, and the three children and the Wish Fairy walked along the tightrope, swung through the air and then jumped down into the trapeze. The crowd all cheered. Soon they were back home in their garden.

Harry, Tracey and Charlie all said, 'Thank you for a lovely day, Wish Fairy! Come back again soon!'

On Top Of The World

Opal Innsbruk

'Tell us a story, Granny.'

Granny could tell such wonderful stories, better even than Mum or Dad, so Jennifer and Scott were full of excited anticipation as they snuggled down under the duvet. (Granny always let them snuggle down in the same bed, usually Jennifer's, while she told a story.)

'Maybe I will and maybe I won't,' said Granny teasingly. 'It depends on which story you want to hear and whether I can remember it or not.'

'Tell us a new one, one that we haven't heard before,' said the children.

'Well now, it just so happens that a story came into my head on the way over here. that I think you would like to hear,' she replied.

'Yes, yes,' cried the children in unison.

Granny drew a chair over to the bedside and settled herself into it.

Here is the story she told.

'In the time when your granny was a little girl, there lived a group of children in a tenement building in a cobblestone street. Now, these children were very poor in a material sense because it was just after a long and terrible war so nobody had anything much, but they were very rich in the things that mattered most. These children were loved. They had enough to eat most days. They had the companionship of one another and oh, what exciting adventures they had together!

One such adventure began on a summer evening after dinner when the children congregated together in the back court, as they usually did, to decide what to play at.

Before going any further, I had better tell you something about the children so you will have a picture of them in your mind as the story unfolds.

There were ten kids of about the same age who usually hung about together. Janey was short and fat; Janet, her younger sister, who was shorter but not so fat; Sarah, their cousin, who was short, fair-haired and slim; June, who lived in a house on the veranda and was tall with brown hair; Maria, who was tall, thin and had black hair; Trevor, Bernie and Susan who were brothers and sister and lived in a tenement across the courtyard; Rita and John, twins who lived in the flat below Janey and Janet, and lastly, Pearl and Babs, older sisters of Maria.

These were the ones who gathered in the courtyard that evening.

'Let's play skipping ropes,' offered Susan.

'No way,' answered Trevor, 'that's a girls' game.'

So the playmates agreed that they would have to choose something they could all play.

'I know, let's climb the dykes,' someone said.

Now I don't know if these children had come from Holland originally where dykes are stone walls built to stop the land being flooded by rising seas, or if their ancestors were, but that was the word they used when referring to any stone wall or stone-constructed shelter.

'Aye! Aye, that's a good idea,' said Pearl and they all agreed, except the twins who said they would have to go home in half an hour.

Then Janet and Sarah said they wanted to exchange scraps and couldn't be bothered climbing, and Susan and Bernie's mother called them from out of her top-floor window to come home.

As the six who were left made their way through to the next courtyard, Bobby, a boy who was slightly older than the others, came down the veranda stairs and called out to them, 'Where are you off to?'

But as climbing over the rooftops was not looked on kindly by the adults, they had to wait until he caught up with them before they replied, 'We're going climbing, coming?'

'OK,' he answered and so one more was added to the expedition.

Stopping at the point of ascent, the group had a whispered discussion as to how they would negotiate the first hazard they always encountered when climbing - Mrs Napier's window. If this hurdle was not passed safely then the climb would be off. It was agreed that Trev would go first as he was the best climber and had more experience of dodging Mrs Napier's eagle eye. If he got past her window undetected and onto the first rooftop, then the rest would follow one by one.

Luckily it was not raining that day so it would be easy to get across the slated roof without, as sometimes happened when it was wet, slipping down the glacier onto the cobblestone yard below.

So up went Trevor ... up the iron pole onto the veranda and over the railings, then onto the roof right beside the old lady's window. Crouching down, he tiptoed under the window, climbed quietly to the top of the roof, crept along a few yards to where the clifftop ended and dropped down the twenty odd feet of the precipice onto the roof below. He'd made it!

When the others, waiting below, saw him vanish over the edge, they formed themselves into a line under the veranda in order of seniority. Bobby first, then Babs, Pearl, Janey, Maria and June.

As Bobby was about to jump onto the pole, a loud, gruff voice reached their ears. 'Come on you two ... your mother wants help with the housework,' and after a token objection, Pearl and Babs left with their father.

Soon they were out of sight and Bobby began to climb the pole. He was as successful as Trevor and he too dropped out of sight.

The procedure was always the same; they always waited until the preceding one was safely over the glacier and down the precipice before the next one began to climb the pole and it was no different today. One by one they all made it safely over, until there was only June left below.

The reason for the safe passing of the window became clear to June when she was halfway up the pole. She caught sight of Mrs Napier approaching the stairs to the veranda carrying shopping bags. She had been out shopping.

Oh no, thought June, *I'll have to wait until she goes in the house before I can start to climb, then hope she doesn't see me.* She waited quietly under the veranda until Mrs Napier had climbed the stairs, walked along the veranda and entered her house before she went up, following the same path the others had taken, until she came to the window where she stopped to listen. Not a sound. Over the railing she went and down onto the roof under the window. Then, crouching down, she listened again. Still no sound, so she began to move along the roof.

Almost at the top, she was stopped in her tracks by the squeaking sound of a window being raised.

'June McIntyre ... you come down off that roof at once!' screamed the old woman. 'Come down this minute!' she called.

June wavered. Should she do as the old woman asked, or should she ignore her and go on?

The children waiting on the roof below, hearing this altercation and seeing June directly above them, called to her, 'Come on June ... jump!'

Making a split-second decision, she dropped down beside them and they took off like hares onto the next rooftop, down a precipice, then veritably flew over the plateaux of several rooftops.

Well out of sight of the harridan, the expedition stopped to rest on a ledge.

'Whew, that was a close call,' wheezed Janey.

'I'll get whacked when I get home,' whispered June, her voice trembling a little. 'She'll tell my parents.'

'Just say it wasn't you,' volunteered Trev.

'Or say you were going after your wee brother or something,' said Maria.

The friends sat here quietly for a while, lost in thought ... contemplating the fate that awaited June and trying to think of a way out for her.

'You won't tell the truth now, will you June?' asked Bobby. 'You won't tell on us?'

'No, I'll think of something. Anyway, it's worth a telling off or a whacking,' grinned June, and the rest giggled in agreement.

'How far will we go today? Will we go past the jumps?' asked Janey.

'We'll see when we come to them,' answered Maria.

They all knew Janey had never yet found the courage to jump the jumps and had always had to turn back alone as the rest went over and onwards. Maybe today would be different.

Sitting there for a while longer, the friends, in turn, sang songs, told stories and jokes until, having used up all their repertoires, they sat once again in companionable silence.

There, high above the noise, dust and bustle of the world below, they dreamed their dreams.

'Let's go,' said Bobby, the undisputed leader, and off they went to tackle the next obstacle they would have to surmount - a sheer brick wall about twenty feet high. Previously when they had attempted this climb they had found it impossible, but with the assistance of a hammer and chisel on subsequent attempts, they now had some grips on the way up; but it was still a formidable task.

Maria went first for, as she was one of the ones to chisel out the grips, she knew best where they were so could scale the wall in double-quick time, which she did. The rest of the team followed one by one, calling out encouragements or insults whenever someone slipped or couldn't find the next grip. Eventually they all reached the top.

They were in no hurry now so they sauntered along blethering to one another until, after several climbs up and down walls, they came to the jumps.

Even for those with previous experience of the jumps it was still a dangerous leap which could, if not judged accurately, be a leap into infinity. So they all stood there on the edge of the fifty-foot drop, psyching themselves up for the leap of faith. The gap was only about six feet wide, not really very far to jump across but it was the thought of the seemingly bottomless pit they would fall into if they landed short that was scary.

Then Bobby walked back a few yards, adopted a runner's starting line stance, took a deep breath and shot forward like an arrow from a bow covering the few yards to the edge of the precipice and jumped.

Sailing in a beautiful arc over the gap, he landed on his feet at the other side.

'Come on, Trev, you next!' he called.

'Wait a minute 'til I tighten my sannies!' Trevor shouted, and bending down at his starting point, he tied the laces of his sandshoes together. 'Here I come!' And with that, he took the same run and leap as Bobby had and landed beside him.

June followed next, but did not land on her feet as the boys had done, but with her tummy hitting the parapet, knocking the wind out of her. When she'd scrambled onto the flat roof, Maria followed. Now they were all over, except Janey.

'Are you going to jump or not?' shouted Maria.

Janey stood there deliberating: should she try it or turn back and go home alone as she had so many times before? Would this be the day she conquered her fear? 'Oh, I don't know,' Janey said, half to herself.

The others heard her and called back, 'Oh, we're away ... see you later,' and they walked away.

Janey watched their backs receding further and further away and something came over her. I'm not saying the fear left her, but she suddenly ran to the edge, leaped over the pit and landed safely on the other side. She couldn't believe she had done it! Looking down in the pit for a second or two she then turned and ran like the wind to catch up with the group. 'I've done it ... I've done it!' she called excitedly as she drew nearer her friends.

They could hardly believe it either! With much shouting of, 'That's great, Janey!' and, 'Well done!' they danced around in a celebratory circle with Janey in the middle.

So surprised and delighted were they at this unexpected turn of events that they abandoned the roof climbing for the day and headed home, laughing and joking with one another all the way.

Janey was on top of the world.'

'What happened when they got home, Granny?' Scott asked. 'What did the other children think ... what did they say?'

'Now, that's a story for another day,' said Granny and kissed them both goodnight.

'Come back soon, Granny,' Jennifer whispered and Granny whispered that she would.

Special

S Mullinger

'Don't go into the shed,' Jill's dad repeated before he left for work.

Wonder why not? thought Jill as she was finishing her breakfast. Jill was recovering from chicken pox. Her mum said next week she could return to school.

'Mum, later on, can I go and play in the garden?' Jill pleaded. 'Looks like it will be a dry day. Promise I'll put my coat on and come indoors if I feel unwell.'

'Well,' said Mum, 'once the sun is shining on the back garden, you could go out in the fresh air, won't do you any harm. Do not go into the garden shed.'

During the next couple of hours, Jill amused herself, completing a jigsaw and reading a book. Finally, Mum said, 'Jill, you can go outside now, while I finish my housework.'

Opening the back door, Jill thought it strange that she was not supposed to go in the shed. She had never been told that before, but both her dad and mum had said it. Why? Only one way to find out, Jill realised as she walked quickly down the garden path. She hoped her mum would not see her as she reached the wooden building.

Jill, aged eight, did not like disobeying her parents. She was an adored only child. At five, she was told she was adopted. Her parents had chosen her and she had lived with them since she was six months of age. Jill did not want to hurt them but she was curious, her parents were acting oddly! Although she loved her mum, she was definitely Dad's little princess. When he arrived home from work, Jill often ran helter-skelter into his outstretched arms.

Jill looked around as she approached the shed. *Perhaps I'll go and stand by it, won't go in.* Of course, when Jill reached the shed, she knew she would go inside. To the right of the wooden door was a large flower tub, placed on two bricks. Underneath it, Dad kept the key for the shed. Jill soon grasped the key in her slim fingers and unlocked the padlock. There might be something dangerous in the shed, like a wild animal. *Don't be silly, Jill,* she thought, *it will be all right.* The door open, she entered the shed.

It was dark inside because the shed was placed in a corner of the garden, in the shade of an old tree. It took a while for Jill's eyes to adjust to the darkness. She remembered her dad kept a torch on the workbench. Reaching out she found the torch, she could not risk turning on the lamp in case Mum saw the light. Jill turned on the torch and closed the door. She looked around but everything seemed the same. Sometimes Jill helped her dad in the shed, but what was different? Dad's work tools all appeared to be in the correct places. her dad's battered armchair was in the corner of the shed. Then she saw it.

A small piece of paper stuck on the set of drawers where Dad kept boxes of nails and screws. This small piece of paper contained many groups of letters handwritten in black ink.

'Ot og
nehctik eht
eht ot txen
napecuas egral
erusaert eht dnif.'

What did that mean? Why didn't her parents want her to see this piece of paper?

Jill had been able to read before she started school. Her reading age was well above average but she could not read the handwritten words. Perhaps it was a foreign language. Jill had learnt some French at school but these words did not look like those words. *If I take the paper with me,* thought Jill, *Mum and Dad will know I have seen it. I could copy out the words and try and work out what they mean.*

Coming out of the shed looking towards the house, Jill was glad to see Mum busy in the kitchen. Good, whatever Mum was doing, she was not watching her daughter.

When Jill opened the back door her mum called, 'Are you OK love? I'm baking a cake for tea, better not come in here, flour dust everywhere. It might make your asthma bad.'

'All right, Mum, came indoors for a pencil and paper. I'll draw a picture for Dad and give it to him at lunch.'

In her bedroom, Jill found an old school book with several empty pages. Perfect. Taking a pencil from her pencil case, Jill headed back to the shed and the mysterious piece of paper.

After copying the weird groups of letters into her book, Jill remembered to re-lock the shed. She returned the keys to under the plant pot. Now her parents would not know she had disobeyed them.

As she walked up the garden path, Jill could not understand why she was not supposed to go in the shed. What was all the secrecy about? It wasn't like her parents to have secrets. She had to find out what was going on. Sitting on a plastic patio garden chair, Jill stared at the written letters. She looked for a long time but could not understand what they meant. More importantly, why did her parents not want her to see them?

Jill heard her dad talking in the kitchen - must be lunchtime! Her dad managed the local post office in the village, a few minutes walk from home. Jill heard him ask, 'Has she worked it out yet?'

'No, not yet,' Mum said.

'Funny! I thought she'd have found it by now,' replied Dad.

Now Jill was confused. What was she supposed to find? Why was she told to stay away from the shed? *Nothing makes any sense,* thought Jill, shaking her head from side to side.

'Jill,' her mother shouted, 'please wash your hands, time for lunch. We'll eat in the kitchen today.'

That's odd, Jill remarked to herself, *we always have lunch in the dining room.*

In the bathroom, Jill put down her book and pencil on the side of the bath. Perhaps the people downstairs were not her parents, but people impersonating her parents. They were in a strange mood. Grabbing her book and turning towards the bathroom cabinet to make sure her face was clean, Jill suddenly laughed aloud. by turning towards the mirror, she was able to easily read the words, which had been written backwards. Jill hurriedly wrote down the message because her mother was shouting that her lunch was getting cold.

During the meal, Mum asked if Jill had given Dad his picture.

'Oh no!' Jill replied. 'Decided to do something else, forgot about the picture. I'll do one this afternoon.'

After the meal, Jill tried to find a way of staying in the kitchen. Her parents kept putting obstacles in her way. Dad suggested the two of them have a game of cards before he returned to work. Mum decided it was time she did the washing up. Jill offered to help but was told no and Mum took ages.

Jill was getting impatient, she wanted to find out if the message was correct. She realised looking in the bathroom she knew what the words spelt. 'Go to the kitchen, next to the large saucepan, find the treasure'.

Wonder what treasure is hidden in the saucepan cupboard? Jill thought. *It cannot be very big.*

Mum said, 'Think I'll read the newspaper Dad brought home.' Looking at her husband, she suggested it was time he went to work and gave him a wink.

Jill had an idea. 'Mum, can I have a drink of squash please? I'll get it myself.'

Mum agreed and Jill ran along the hall, into the kitchen.

Closing the door behind her, Jill knelt down by the saucepan cupboard. There beside the largest saucepan was a small red rectangular box - the treasure. Attached to the box was a piece of paper with the words, 'Please wear this afternoon at your birthday party'. Inside the box was a silver heart-shaped locket.

'At last,' said Dad, as both he and Mum, who had entered the kitchen smiled broadly at Jill.

'Wondered if we had made the clue too difficult for you,' Jill's mum said, 'because we had to cancel your birthday party ten days ago, we've rearranged it for this afternoon.'

Jill ran to her dad, then her mum and gave them both a hug.

Mum continued, 'Your dad delivered the new invitations one morning on his way to work. Your friend's parents have been visiting the post office with acceptance slips for the last few days. Becky's the only friend not coming, her mum phoned to say Becky and her baby brother have chickenpox.'

Jill said, 'That's one problem solved, explains why you've been acting very peculiar today. Oh! by the way, the locket is beautiful.'

'Just like you sweetheart,' replied Dad. 'Promise me that you will help Mum this afternoon. There's work to be done in preparation for your party including blowing up balloons and putting birthday banners everywhere. I really must go back to work, see you later, my two special girls,' Dad said, blowing them a kiss each before leaving the house.

The afternoon passed quickly. Jill was given the job of filling the party bags for her friends. Mum blew up the balloons, Jill tied them into bunches. She held them ready for Mum to hang from the ceiling. Jill attached pieces of Sellotape to birthday banners, which she put on doors and on the stair banisters. Once all the decorations were in place, Jill had a wash and put on her party clothes plus new locket. Mum disappeared into her bedroom and reappeared laden down with various kinds of crisps, biscuits and pop. She left the centre of the dining room table bare until minutes before the party was to begin. Carefully from the kitchen Mum carried a large cake in the shape of a butterfly. She placed it on the empty spot.

'Oh Mum!' said Jill, rushing to give her a kiss, 'that explains what you were doing this morning in the kitchen - it's fabulous! But can I ask you something?'

'Yes dear, what is it?' replied Mum.

Jill said, 'Why did you and Dad tell me to stay away from the shed?'

'We knew,' answered Mum, 'if we told you not to go in the shed - you would be curious and be sure to want to know what was hidden inside. Realising you are almost better and are getting bored at home, we thought as well as your surprise party, we would create a little adventure for you. This would keep you out of my way, then I could concentrate on making your cake. You will also have something to tell your friends when they arrive.'

Just as Mum finished speaking the door bell chimed announcing the arrival of the first party guest. Jill's dad arrived during the party. He took several photographs for the family album.

Later that evening, laying in her bed, looking at her locket on her bedside cabinet, Jill realised she was a very lucky girl. She had perfect parents. They called her their special daughter but they were her extra special parents. With that thought, Jill closed her eyes on a strange but wonderful day.

Next-Door's Cat

Ivy Allpress

Next-door's cat was a very positive cat. When she slipped out, she would march up and down imperiously, mewing incessantly and demanding to be noticed and loved. She trotted after everybody, the whole world was her friend and must receive her rapturous overtures. She had a different character to my cat who was soft, cuddly and rather vague and gentle except where mice were concerned.

Next-door's cat was a rather smart tabby with bright green eyes which lit up like lamps in the winter gloom, and she wanted to know what was in everybody's shopping bags as they walked away from the corner shop.

The corner shop was a great institution and a meeting place for all the gossips. Many a problem was thrashed out there, and just as many created. It was a boon to women coming home from work in the evenings. They could buy their odds and ends of shopping there and unburden themselves of the problems of the day to the kindly proprietress and to each other, and they would go away feeling that they were not alone in having a problem. The local worthies irreverently called the little meeting place 'The Cat's Club' which was entirely erroneous as most of the women were kindly disposed towards their fellow creatures.

Alas the shop is no more, and it is sadly missed. It was the usual story. The owner was bought out by developers who did not develop and the once thriving little shop soon became derelict.

Getting back to the cat, I shall never forget the time that she went missing.

We all searched high and low, and were forced to the reluctant conclusion that she had either been run over or stolen.

We asked the road sweeper if he had seen a little tabby cat lying in the gutter, he said he had not but promised to look out for her. The postman and the milkman were also pressed into service as were the various insurance men that collected in that part of the road. Someone even asked the rent collector which made a change from the usual enquiries as to when the roof was going to be repaired or the guttering fixed.

The search went on for days, and to make it worse we were haunted by a continuous plaintive mewing and we could not trace it. It seemed to be changing direction all the time. The men were dismissive and decided that the sound was our fancy or the wind and we had better resign ourselves to the fact that the cat had gone. This we could not do, we were more determined than ever to find her and to track down that tantalising noise. After all, we figured if it was not the little tabby that had got herself into bother it must be some other cat in trouble.

The children thought that the sound was coming from the empty shop and they could get in quite easily round the back. Well, as we did not know the whereabouts of the new owner of the shop, in the name of kindness to animals we would have to investigate the persistent mewing ourselves.

The slimmest of us managed to squeeze round the broken door round the back. What a scene of devastation met our eyes. The little shop that had been so trim and neat had been vandalised past description. The former owner would have wept if she could have seen what had had happened to her shop.

The plaintive cries seemed to be coming from some broken floorboards. We pulled them apart and somebody produced a torch. We felt a momentary gleam of hope. Then someone said that it was a black cat, and so it was, accompanied by five tiny kittens. She was trapped under the floorboards by a piece of broken wood which had fallen across.

We moved the board and a saucer of milk and some cat food was provided. The mother cat got up, shook her little family aside and gratefully accepted the meat and milk then she settled down with her family again, full up and contentedly purring.

There was much debating as to what was to be done with them.

Twice daily the crime of breaking and entering was committed in the name of kindness to animals, especially cats. The kittens grew and flourished and were beginning to explore the shop and even further. The time was fast approaching when homes would have to be found for them. People came and inspected them and selections were made.

Eventually all the kittens were found homes and the mother cat was adopted by the mistress of the little cat that went missing. Yes, she did turn up again, appearing as mysteriously as she had vanished. Where she had been all those weeks we will never know, but she was just the same little tabby cat, demanding, imperious, inquisitive and loving as ever.

A Day In Gracie's Garden

Peggy Finch

It was a fine sunny day and Gracie was playing in her garden, she had been playing on the slide and the swing, but was now feeling a bit bored.

Gracie lay down on a rug that her mummy had left on the grass, as she did Prince came over and stretched out beside her. Prince was the family pet, a black Labrador dog who was six years old, just one year younger than Gracie. While Gracie had been on the swing she had seen Prince scratching at his collar, he did not like wearing one when it was hot.

As they both rested on the rug Gracie thought she heard a musical sound and it seemed to be coming from Prince, she kept very still and quiet, listening carefully and heard the sound again, yes it was a song. Gracie moved her head nearer to Prince and as she did the song got louder and this is what she heard:-

'If I were a flea and free
I would travel the world on a donkey's knee
We would jog up and down, all around town
Then call in at Tina's for tea.'

Gracie looked all around but could not see anyone in the garden, but she knew it was not her singing, perhaps her mummy had the radio on? She would run indoors to see.

All of a sudden Prince scratched at his collar again, as he did Gracie heard a tiny 'hooray' and could see a flea sitting on the rug. As she watched he started to sing the song again, then as the song finished he nodded to Gracie, took one huge hop onto the grass and was gone! Gracie rubbed her eyes, not knowing if she could believe what she had seen, perhaps Prince had heard the song too. Just as Gracie was going to ask him, her eyes rested on a big red rose in the flower bed. No I don't believe it! A bee was humming and gathering pollen from the rose when all of a sudden the bee started to sing!

'If I were a bee and free
I would travel the world with my honey sack
Go to Timbuktu on a camel's back
Visiting flowers all the way there and back.'

Gracie was amazed! She had often listened to the bees buzzing from flower to flower but never had she heard a bee sing! As she watched wide-eyed the bee seemed to smile at her, then suddenly flew over the rose bush up into the blue sky and out of sight.

Prince was asleep and dreaming, Daddy had told Gracie that dogs make funny noises sometimes as they sleep, it was no good asking him if he had seen or heard anything.

Gracie thought about all the things that she had seen. Had she imagined that the flea wore a hat just like a jester's on his head? The hat was long and pointed, at one end, with a bright yellow and red diamond pattern, there was a small bell on the pointed end which made a tinkling sound as he hopped, she thought of the lovely sound it would make as the flea jogged up and down on the donkey's knee.

Remembering all that had happened, Gracie thought hard about the bee, she was sure that the bee had been wearing a crown! At school she had been taught that there was a queen bee in every hive and was feeling really pleased that she had seen one actually wearing her crown!

Once again Gracie heard the music, had the flea or the bee returned to the garden? No! this time the song was coming from the old oak tree, there it was again! It was a blackbird sitting on a branch and he was singing:-

'I am a bird and free

I travel the world flying from tree to tree

Singing my song as I travel alone

Many wonders to see on my way home.'

This time Gracie was not surprised at all by the bird singing, all different birds sang their songs in the garden, she was puzzled however by the fact that all of them, the fleas, the queen bee and the blackbird seemed to know the same song but with different words.

What a magical time Gracie had spent on the rug in her garden, she was wondering about all that had happened when she heard her mummy calling out, 'It's time for tea.'

Prince and Gracie raced each other to the kitchen door and as she took her mummy's hand, she asked, 'Where is Timbuktu, Mummy?'

'Why would you ask me that?' said her mum.

Gracie took the whole of teatime to tell her story, careful not to miss out any detail. After she had finished her mummy just smiled and said how special she was to have such a wonderful dream!

Later that day, after Gracie had bathed and got into bed she remembered her special time in the garden and wondered, was there a world of songs and rhymes that only special children could hear, or have we just got to listen more carefully to the world around us?

Arachnid And Me On Our Initial Space Journey

Maureen Dawson

One day when I was alone in our family garden shed I spied a large spider, he was no ordinary spider. His eight legs seemed to be beckoning me to him. I looked all around me to make sure no one else had followed me into the garden shed.

When I realised that there was only the spider and myself in the shed I trembled but those spider legs were still beckoning me to come over.

I closed the garden shed door ever so gently that no one else would see that I was inside the shed. I wanted to be alone with this spider.

When I got the shed door closed I saw that the spider had black and white stripes on its body and its legs looked even bigger now.

'Hello spider,' I whispered very softly, and crept up beside him, I was trembling.

'My name is Arachnid,' said the spider and he put is eight legs around me and tucked me into his web, it was a large wheel-like web and it had spokes but the centre piece that I moved into was very sticky, I realised then I was trapped.

'Please Arachnid, release me and let me go,' I cried very softly in a trembling voice. But when I tried to pull away from the sticky centre-piece Arachnid just grew and grew. He was even bigger than me now, and I am now a big boy, five years of age.

'Come with me,' he said, 'and we shall have some fun, will you?'

I nodded yes but I was too afraid to speak.

The orb or web that was around me suddenly turned into a helicopter and the roof lifted off the garden shed.

Arachnid got into the pilot's seat, pressed a button and a large propeller started turning round and round.

Away we went into the air, I thought, *I just can't wait until I see my friends and tell them about this adventure.*

Just then Arachnid moved out of his pilot seat and said, 'You drive now.'

I could not believe what was happening but I moved into his seat and took the controls and away we went even faster than before.

'We are going to see some space people,' Arachnid said, turning his head towards me and his eight eyes shone down on me.

Into the unknown we went, passing over all the clouds driving along with and above the airplanes.

Next a large cloud appeared and Arachnid said, 'This will be our stop,' and he moved me over to the passenger seat again. He then landed the helicopter on a space station but we could not get out because we were not wearing spacesuits.

I was annoyed and I started to cry and sob because I had always wanted to be a real spaceman.

Arachnid then said, 'On my undersides I have organs called spinnerets with which I can make silk. This silk is first a liquid and is manufactured in certain glands in my body, I can make it into parachutes and lifelines to save myself if I fall, now that I am very large I could make spacesuits for you and me.' He then released me from his web and told me to sleep for a while and stop that silly crying and sobbing. That is exactly what I did do.

After a long sleep I could hear Arachnid's voice say, 'Wake up now, your spacesuit and mine are both ready.' There was excitement in his voice.

I could not believe what I saw when I opened my eyes, there was Arachnid in the most beautiful spacesuit I had ever seen and one exactly the same sitting beside him for me. I hastily put it on and then we both got out of our helicopter immediately.

All we could see was spaceships and everyone working away in spacesuits, they did not even stop to speak to us. I was very disappointed.

Arachnid turned to me and said, 'I forgot about having to make an appointment before coming here,' and he disappeared for a short time.

When he came back he had a smile on his face and he told me that he had made an appointment to come back soon but it would be another surprise for me.

Arachnid and I both got into our helicopter and he said, 'Will you pilot us home.'

'Of course I will,' I said with a gleam in my eye.

After a while Arachnid said to me, 'Will you give me the controls now? I wish to make another landing before we reach home.'

I moved over and Arachnid took the controls and said, 'I would like to stop soon, my spider cousin makes silk houses and I know that he would let you and me store our spacesuits in one of his houses.'

New Fiction - Hickory Dickory

I took my spacesuit off and then moved over to the driving seat again to let Arachnid take his spacesuit off too.

After taking his spacesuit off he put the two suits together and moved to the pilot seat again.

'Oh, we just have changed in good time, we will now land on the desert below, this is where my spider cousin lives.'

I looked out and I could see herds of camels and gazelle in the desert . . .

Arachnid told me to close my eyes and to keep them closed until he told me to open them again.

I could hear noises but I did not dare to peep because I knew that Arachnid would be annoyed with me and I was depending on him to take me home again.

After a while Arachnid said, 'Open your eyes, get set, away we go,' and we soared up above the clouds again.

I was so happy and I did not want this space adventure to end.

After a time I knew our helicopter was making its way down and we were going home again.

I thought I heard my name being called now, it seemed that it was coming louder and louder. I then recognised the voice, it was the voice of my mother.

Arachnid gave one big sneeze and he shrank into his original size again and the sticky centre piece and the web that was holding me disappeared and I was free again.

Mum opened the garden shed door just at that minute and said, 'So here you are and I have been looking everywhere for you. Your dinner is ready, now come along.'

'But Mum I have had a great time, I have been away to space, in a helicopter and I was the pilot sometimes. Arachnid and I are going back another day because Arachnid made a proper appointment for the next time.'

Mum just laughed and said, 'Would Arachnid take me too? I would love to go.'

The Ghosts Of Christmas Past

Neil Wesson

The house was completely in darkness, all was prepared for the following day. Outside the sky was clear and the moon shone full and bright. The straggling partygoers were now a little thin on the ground at this late hour, as thin as the light dusting of snow that had fallen an hour earlier.

All over the world children and adults alike slept, dreaming of the following morning's revelry, all was prepared.

In the living room of a house sat a bureau. Normally throughout the year it served as a purely functional piece of furniture, but now, in the season of advent, it had become the focal point of the room. On it sat a small plastic tree decorated with silver and red glass baubles. A string of green beads also hung from its branches, as did a collection of twinkling lights, now turned off for the night.

Either side of the holly-adorned fireplace stood two green and red felt-lined sacks both bursting full of parcels, brightly wrapped.

The old Christmas tree had seen it all before of course, it knew that the following morning it would hear the words, 'He's been!' as two excited young boys would both see the empty glass and plate in the dining room, not to mention the well-chewed carrot top which always accompanied Santa's fare.

Seconds after that the living room door would spring open and the unwrapping would commence. The ritual was the same every year; presents, trying to get the youngsters dressed, then the smell, oh the smell of the cooking dinner.

All that was yet to come, still several hours away.

The little tree thought back over the years, how many presents had it seen unwrapped, too numerous to remember, some though he could not forget, some long gone for whatever reason. Worn out through overuse or disposed of because of neglect, some would stay here always.

The time was fast approaching now, it usually happened at the stroke of three. The clock on the mantelpiece read two fifty-five, still five minutes to go.

A thud broke the silence of the night. The baubles on the tree let out the slightest jingle as they gently touched each other, was it vibration from the activities upstairs or was it the tree curiously looking around?

Listening hard, the tree heard a slight cry from one of the boys, then silence once more. Obviously one of the over-excited children dreaming, not surprising really as this was Christmas Eve.

Once again calm fell over the house as it did over most of the village, not to mention the world. Then something happened, without the slightest hint of anything untoward a blue and red ball, the size of a tennis ball rolled across the floor.

The tree smiled to itself, the yearly trip through nostalgia was about to commence. From one side of the room a robot, not unlike an android from a popular 50s American TV show, crackled and fizzed across the floor. In the other direction coming to meet it was an old racing car, sticking out of its brightly coloured shell turned a clockwork driven key.

Bouncing down from somewhere unseen came a wooden hoop. The tree didn't remember this present long disregarded, the Jack-in-the-box took his mind elsewhere as it sprang open. Both of these long gone toys were from a different time, another generation. The old play things were followed by a wooden spinning top. It stopped, toppled over then silently disappeared.

A doll, blonde wiry curls filling her head appeared. She was in a pushchair being paraded around the room. While the pram lapped the room once again an armed vehicle drove into the middle of the floor, a male doll dressed in army attire sat in the driver's seat.

More and more toys appeared shimmering in and out of existence, all overlapping but not interfering with one another.

The table football game stood in the middle of the room, as did the snooker table. On the floor building blocks of various designs and ages formed together to make cars, ships and spacecraft, before dismantling themselves and reforming into other sculptures. Police cars, fire engines and ambulances criss-crossed the floor, some of them with light flashing some without.

Watching over all of the toys from years gone by was a larger orange ball, two ribbed horns protruding from its top, on its surface a large smiling face. It was of course a Space Hopper. Like the tree, he had seen it all and watched with a quiet calm about himself.

As the clock struck four all fell silent once again. Only the tree remained.

In an hour or so this year's presents would be unwrapped and played with. He wondered which toys would be favoured?

At five thirty a bump was heard from the upstairs, this was quickly followed by excited voices. Moments later the thump, thump of feet coming down the stairs could be heard. The door burst open and two excited boys burst into the room followed by two bleary-eyed parents.

The eldest of the two climbed onto the arm of the sofa and flicked on the light switch.

Joy appeared on the young faces, 'He's been, look Jake, he's been!' said Sam to his young brother.

The first and biggest present opened that morning was a Space Hopper.

Strange how these things come around, thought the tree allowing itself a little smile, after all no one was looking.

The Mystery Of The Missing Necklace

Angela Bradley

Danny was sitting on his usual stool in *Witicombe's World of Wisdom*, when the bell jangled loudly, the shop door burst open, and Mortella Styx strode in.

'Out of my way, boy,' she shrieked as she pushed past him.

'Well, have you found it?' she demanded as she glared at the shaking figure of Jacob Witicombe.

'No . . . no, n-not y-yet,' he stammered.

'Well you'd better hurry up,' she shrieked, 'or I will have to think of something really nasty to do to you.'

Danny knew she would too, for she was a mean and very ugly woman with her squinty eyes, bristly chin and fat, warty nose. She turned to leave and saw him staring at her. 'Open the door then, you gawping pop-eyed toad.'

Better do it, he thought, and reached for the handle.

Kicking out at Jacob's bristling ginger cat she manoeuvred her huge body through the door, squeezed her thin lips together and snarled like an angry she-wolf.

Jacob sat down. He looked very worried. Picking up the terrified cat he stroked her gently until she eventually curled up and went to sleep.

'You alright Danny?' he asked, sighing.

''Course I am,' said Danny bravely. 'Mortella Styx doesn't frighten me.'

'Well she should do,' said Jacob. 'She's evil through and through. Just remember that.'

'But what is she looking for?'

'The necklace - Bella's necklace, of course. As soon as she saw it she wanted to steal it.'

Danny started to think about Bella, who was Jacob's daughter and his best friend. They'd grown up together. Danny had always preferred to be here in this dusty old bookshop than in his own mum and dad's fish and chip shop next door.

But a few weeks ago, something terrible had happened. Bella had walked out of the door and disappeared.

The police had searched everywhere but they couldn't find her. Poor Jacob had been awfully upset. He missed her so much, so did

Danny. He remembered how thrilled she'd been on her last birthday when Jacob had given her the beautiful diamond necklace that had belonged to her dead mother. She'd loved it so much that she had worn it all the time.

When Mortella had seen it she'd been green with envy. Her nasty black eyes had glittered greedily as she'd stared at the sparkling gems. Because of this Jacob was certain that she'd had something to do with Bella's disappearance.

Danny felt very sorry for the old man and when he'd found the half-starved ginger cat on the doorstep he'd asked Jacob to look after it. Perhaps helping the cat would give him something else to think about.

Meanwhile, Danny decided to try and find Bella himself, even if it meant that he had to come face to face with Mortella.

People said that she lived in a large house in the forest. Maybe Bella was imprisoned there, but, if Mortella had kidnapped her and found that she wasn't wearing the necklace, what would she have done with her?

So one day, feeling extremely nervous he set off to search the thick, dark forest. *If I keep to the path,* he thought, *I'll be able to find my way back.*

He didn't like the quiet gloominess or the closeness of the trees. He knew there was hidden life all around him, animals, birds and creepy crawlies, but he couldn't see them.

Startled by some rustling sounds he began to run, but tripped over a tree root and fell down. 'Ouch!' he cried as he got up, rubbing his knee. His heart began to beat frantically. He peered ahead of him. He really wanted to go back - but he knew that he had to go on.

At last the light started to show through the trees and he felt grass beneath his feet as he walked out into a sunny clearing. In the centre stood an old, tumbledown cottage. There were holes in the roof and broken glass in the windows.

He stood for a few minutes watching and listening for any signs of life from inside - but the place seemed deserted. He crept forward and peeped in. He realised that it was just the shell of a house. No one had lived there for years, certainly not Mortella.

Now what shall I do, he thought. *I've no food or water. I've walked miles through this ghostly forest and found nothing. Shall I go on, or turn round and go back?*

He sat down in the sunshine and leant his back against the wall. He felt so weary. He knew that it was dangerous to go to sleep. Forests were full of wild, hungry animals, but he was so tired, so . . .

What an awful dream he was having. Giant spiders were crawling all over him, binding him up in their tough silky webs. He couldn't move his arms and legs. He could hardly breathe. Then he heard the laugh - and his eyes shot open.

There she stood above him, so close that he could see the evil in her vicious, black eyes and the ghastly wart on her ugly, fat nose.

'So, my little snooping bloodhound, I have you in my power,' she chuckled, her fat body shaking disgustingly.

Danny wriggled, as he found himself bound, not by spiders' webs, but tightly with a rope around his hands and feet. 'Let me go,' he shouted. 'You won't get away with this. My dad'll come looking for me.' He sounded much braver than he felt.

'I'll let you go - my little juicy pumpkin,' she said, in a suddenly silken voice, 'when you promise to do something for me in return.'

'What?' asked Danny, realising that she still needed him - alive.

'Find me the necklace. You have two days, and if you don't I will lock you in that miserable little shop and burn it to the ground. I'm sure to find it then.'

'So you think it's hidden in the shop, do you?'

'Well, that little minx wasn't wearing it the day I . . .'

'You did kidnap Bella,' roared Danny, angrily. 'Where is she? What have you done with her?'

'I don't know,' said Mortella. 'She tried to escape. I had to . . .'

'What . . . what did you do to her? You'd better tell me, or - I won't look for the necklace,' said Danny.

'You stupid little worm,' hissed Mortella. 'You are in no position to bargain. You'll do as you're told - or else.'

He hardly noticed the long, dark walk back through the forest. He was so worried about what had happened to Bella. He had to find the necklace, and quickly. Then work out how to deal with Mortella.

Jacob was horrified when Danny told him where he'd been.

'I knew I was right,' he said. 'That dreadful woman has done something awful to my poor Bella, and all because of a necklace. If we find it she can have it. I just want Bella back.'

Danny could see how emotional the poor man was becoming so he said, 'We'd better start looking. We've only got two days.'

So they began. Every book was opened. Drawers and cupboards were emptied. Furniture was moved, but they found nothing. On the evening of the second day they collapsed in desperation as the grandfather clock struck nine.

'The clock,' said Danny, 'we haven't looked in the clock.' He jumped up and opened the small door. Peering inside he saw the glittering necklace hanging behind the ticking pendulum.

'It's here. We've found it,' he laughed happily. 'Bella must have hidden it for safety - from Mortella.'

'But she did not succeed,' came a hard, steely voice, as Mortella wobbled across the room. 'Now give it to me.'

Quicker than a flash of lightning she grabbed the necklace and fastened it round her podgy neck.

As she stood grinning maliciously at them the necklace seemed to tighten. The diamonds, like pointed thorns, started to dig into her flesh. She yelled with pain and fell to the floor, gasping. Her fat, stubby fingers pulled at her throat, trying to wrench away the tightening, throttling band.

Just as it seemed she would surely die, the ginger cat, who had been watching, walked over and pulled the necklace from the red and bleeding neck and sat with it in her mouth.

Mortella staggered to her feet and lurched towards the door.

She was beaten. She knew it, and with one last look of hatred she vanished.

'I think the cat wants to wear the necklace,' said Danny, laughing, and placed it round the purring animal's neck.

Immediately she began to grow and change. Her fur disappeared. She stood up on two legs. Clothes covered her body.

Silky hair hung down onto her shoulders and to their amazed delight Bella's sweet smile appeared on her face - whilst around her neck, the diamond necklace sparkled and gleamed.

Norman Meets The Googliebird

Michelle Hinton

Norman was a funny little fellow. He had masses of curly black hair, a small button nose and beady black eyes. When he smiled, which wasn't often, he had little dimples either side of his mouth, he was also slightly on the chubby side. He was twelve years old, and from the first day he started going to school to the present day, he never had a single friend. It wasn't for lack of trying; the other kids in school thought he was extremely weird in his own little way, so they avoided him like the plague.

On one occasion, Norman was in his maths lesson. All the students were working in total silence and Norman just sat in his chair, he started to move his head from side to side and he kept repeating the words, 'I'm gonna get ya'. He then laughed for no apparent reason, it was like he was in a deep trance and he was oblivious of what he was doing.

This episode scared the whole class; they stared at him with pure terror in their eyes. The maths teacher marched over to Norman and told him to leave the classroom immediately and go and see the headmistress.

'What have I done, Miss? Why are you sending me to the Head's office?' he said with a blank expression.

'You know why, Norman! You will not disturb another one of my lessons with your silly antics. Now off you go,' said Miss Fletchley pointing to the door.

Norman removed himself from class and he had no recollection of what he had done. As he walked by the other desks to leave he looked at Shelley Moshin.

'What are you looking at, Nutty Norman?'

Norman ignored her; he was quite bewildered because he didn't know what he had done wrong. From that day forward Norman was known as the school freak.

As the days flew by, Norman would sometimes stand still in the bustling school corridors and he would rock his body back and forth chanting, 'I'm gonna get ya'. The students soon learnt just to ignore him and they would walk past him pretending he wasn't even there.

Then, one particular day, Norman was doing his normal thing, keeping himself to himself, going from class to class, when he felt a hand on his shoulder, this was the first time anyone had ever touched him; he turned around and saw a girl. He couldn't recall seeing this girl in school before, but the funny thing was the other students totally ignored them both.

'Hello, Norman, I'm so glad to finally meet you, it's taken me ages to find you. My name's Sophia,' she said.

'Oh, er hello. How you know my name?' said Norman with a very puzzled expression on his face.

'Everybody knows your name, silly. You're very popular around here and you're a legend in your own way,' said Sophia with a smile.

'How can I be popular? I'm known as the school freak. You must have the wrong person,' he said. Norman started to walk away quite rapidly.

'Norman, wait a minute, I want to be your friend,' shouted Sophia.

Like a flash of lightning Sophia was standing in front of Norman smiling at him. This scared him a little because he never saw her walk past him.

'I've got to go, I'm going to be late for science,' he said.

'Just follow me Norman. I have something to show you. Come on …' said Sophia, as she grabbed his hand.

Norman tried to break free from her grasp, but she was so strong. She pulled him along the school corridors ignoring his pleas. 'Where are we going? I'm going to get detention for missing my lesson,' he said.

'We're here now,' said Sophia as she came to an abrupt halt outside the school library.

'I haven't got time to go in there and read. I'm late for my lesson.'

'Then tell Mr Periwinkle it was my fault, then you won't get into any trouble. Follow me!' said Sophia excitedly.

Sophia opened the library door and walked in, dragging Norman behind her. He felt strange because when they walked past Mrs Beltway, the school librarian, she didn't say anything; nor did she acknowledge they were there. She stood up and went to close the library door, she muttered to herself, 'I wish it wasn't so windy out there today.'

Norman looked at Sophia and said, 'Why didn't we get questioned about being in here at lesson time? Mrs Beltway didn't even look at us.'

'My dear Norman, don't you stop moaning? Just follow me and all will be revealed my friend,' said Sophia, smiling.

Sophia pulled him along the rows of bookshelves; not realising books were falling off the shelves when they rushed past them. Norman did try and pick them up but Sophia wouldn't let him. He then saw Mrs Beltway bending down and picking up all the books. He really was beginning to get frightened, sweat trickled down his chubby red cheeks.

Sophia stopped in front of a bookcase, which had the history books on. Norman just looked at her strangely.

'Listen to me, when I remove these two books a secret door will open. So just follow me through it,' said Sophia.

'What? You really are strange. Are you sure you're feeling OK? There is no way a secret door will open.'

They stood facing each other. Sophia had her hand on one of the books and Norman was gnawing at his fingernails.

'Hey, Nutty Norman, it's your turn to read your essay,' whispered Bert.

Miss Farthing sat at her desk tapping her foot waiting for Norman to read his essay. When she saw him stand up she said, 'Nice to have you back in reality Norman, please read me your essay.'

He started to read his English essay, and halfway through it Miss Farthing told him to stop and she asked him why he had written an essay on Eskimos when that subject had nothing whatsoever to do with Romeo and Juliet.

Norman looked at her feeling extremely embarrassed and humiliated, his face glowed like ripe tomatoes.

This was another one of Norman's great embarrassing situations, he felt a complete and utter fool.

Sophia had her hand on the second book, and Norman said, 'Well, go on then, remove it. I can't wait to see the so-called secret door.'

Sophia pulled the book out, and Norman couldn't believe his eyes when a yellow door actually appeared. To say he was shocked was an understatement.

'Quickly, Norman, let's go,' said Sophia as she yanked him by his clothes.

They were now standing in a dimly lit, musty smelling corridor. Norman was trembling in fright. 'Where are we …?' he stuttered.

'Don't ask questions, you will understand shortly. Now tread carefully and be quiet,' whispered Sophia.

They started tiptoeing down the corridor, it seemed to go on for miles, and all they could hear were their own footsteps.

'Sophia, where are we going?' said Norman.

'Just down here. Not much further. No wonder I was sent to find you, you never stop talking.'

'What do you mean, you were sent to find me? Who sent you?'

Sophia turned round and looked at him, he was sweating profusely. She said, 'You look so scared. I'm not going to hurt you. Please just follow me and *ssshhh.*'

He did what he was told and he stopped asking questions. They came to the end of the corridor and Sophia asked Norman to say 'Googliebird' three times. He started laughing; this little trip was becoming a joke.

'Googliebird, Googliebird, Goog ...' he said. Norman couldn't finish his sentence because tears were rolling down his face, he was laughing so much.

Sophia wasn't impressed, she stood with her hands on her hips, and she looked like she was chewing a wasp. 'If you're not going to be serious, I'm not taking you further and it will be your loss,' she said scornfully.

'OK, OK, I'm sorry. I will say it again. Googliebird, Googliebird, Googliebird,' he said.

Norman didn't even have the time to ask Sophia what a Googliebird was, a huge talon burst through the wall and he was sucked into the unknown. All that was heard was his screams.

In the school assembly, the headmistress, teachers and all the children were saying a silent prayer. They had heard about Norman's parents being killed in a tragic car accident. The headmistress thought it was appropriate to say a prayer, not just for Norman's parents but also for Norman because he was now an orphan.

Thud. Norman landed on a stone-cold floor and Sophia landed at the side of him.

'What the hell is happening? And what was that thing that carried me here?' he said.

'That was Valens, the Googliebird. Quick, Norman, stand up and look at the carving in the wall. Somebody wants to see you,' ordered Sophia.

Norman stood up and looked at the strange carving, it looked like his father's face. He then felt arms embrace him. His parents were hugging him. He didn't understand, his parents passed away years ago, and now they were suddenly here.

'Mum, Dad, what's happening? I don't understand, what are you doing here?' he said.

His parents let go of him and his mum said, 'My darling baby Norman. It's taken ten years for someone to finally find you, and it was your sister Sophia who has brought you back to us.'

'My sister! Am I dreaming? I was in school going to my science lesson five minutes ago,' he said.

His mum and dad then explained to him that they were all killed In the car accident including Norman.

'So what you're saying is I'm dead and I'm a ghost,' he said.

'Yes Norman you are,' said his dad smiling.

'No, no, I'm not dead. I was in school,' said Norman in a panic-stricken voice.

Sophia then held his hand and said, 'You're not in school anymore, those were flashbacks you were having. That's why nobody could see us in the corridors. And that Mrs Beltway woman couldn't see us in the library. You have been haunting this school for a very long time.'

Norman didn't know what to say, he stood with his arms wrapped around his mum's waist hugging her.

Once Norman got over the initial shock that he was a ghost, Sophia led him back into school and they were so naughty.

They had loads of fun laughing at the students' faces when they scared them by opening and closing the doors and windows. They picked pens up and threw them across the classrooms.

Norman had finally found out where he truly belonged, and he was overjoyed. He was glad to feel loved and his parents treated him like the special boy that he was.

The Belly Button Bears

Susannah Walker

The world of the Belly Button Bears is one amazing one. I'm not going to take you on adventures but I'm going to tell you facts, facts that will shock you.

Didn't you know about the Belly Button Bears? Well I'll start with where they live which, of course, is in everyone's belly button. Their homes spiral down and down with little lanterns lighting up little tubes that are their rooms.

Oh, you say, *but the doctor would see them if they lived in your belly button.* But, oh no, they are not visible to the human eye and too quick to be picked up by a microscope. They have a flap that covers their homes when a doctor is examining a, 'Flippo'? Oh yes, that is what they call humans, 'Flippos'.

They are small bears with athletic bodies. They live for adrenaline rushes, that's why their maximum age is only five years. *Oh peanuts,* you say, well don't worry I will proceed to tell you all about what makes them tick (and that's not a clock).

Now, big people are the Belly Button Bears' guardians. Some big people have schools in their belly buttons, some have churches and police stations. Some larger big people have sports arenas and hospitals. Yes, the Belly Button Bears are like us in a lot of ways.

Now if you're well behaved for at least a year the Belly Button Bears can sprinkle you with flim-flam dust which can magically bring you into the Belly Button Bears' world for one whole day but you will never remember as lam-lam dust is sprinkled onto you before you go back to your world and it erases the memory of your experience with the Belly Button Bears.

If you went for a day, what would you love to do - race fleas, ski, puzzles, gymnastics, hang-gliding, go on safari, decorate, deep-sea dive? You can make up your own mind.

They do have enemies such as dust mites who are always sabotaging their equipment, causing accidents and stealing their trained fleas.

If you have an outer belly button it means the Belly Button Bears have gone on holiday. If you see a belly button piercing with a jewel it means it's a Belly Button Bear's birthday.

They love women who wear loads of make-up because the use this make-up to decorate their homes in lots of different bright colours.

They love people with tattoos, these people make great puzzles and mazes which take a long time to figure out for more intellectual bears.

People who have lots of piercings make great gymnastics where some of the greatest Belly Button Bear gymnasts compete to a high level, twisting, spinning and jumping from hoop to ring and ring to hoop.

Next we have the hairy humans, namely men with beards, the Belly Button Bears love going on safari investigating every area in the gigantic beard.

The favourite human is a woman with waxed legs for the Belly Button Bears have great fun skiing really fast down them and reach amazing speeds of at least 180 specs, this is top speed in Belly Button Bear language.

Tall people are great as the hang-gliding off their head is a source of constant adrenaline rushes for the Belly Button Bears. Another popular pastime is when the Flippo has a bath, great for scuba-diving and deep-sea diving, but I have to say this is a dangerous sport, lots of Belly Button Bears' lives have been lost down the plughole.

Now, when skinny Flippos go to sleep the Belly Button Bears have races riding their prize fleas round and round, but no gambling is allowed, especially in the Belly Button Bears' Gold Cup race. These fleas are especially trained on dogs and are not allowed to bite Flippos, so if you're ever bitten by a flea it is a wild one, untrained by the Belly Button Bears. The fleas are used also to go visiting all other Bears although sometimes they will use spider webs to travel from Flippo to Flippo.

Fluff from your clothes makes Belly Button Bears' clothes. Crumbs that you spill feed the Belly Button Bears for weeks.

The Belly Button Bears pledge to look after their Flippos to the best of their ability because if their Flippo becomes ill there will be no more adrenaline rushes and the Belly Button Bears have to stay in until their Flippo is better. Although they have been known to bungee jump every time a Flippo coughs giving them a massive adrenaline rush as they twang backwards and forwards. All Belly Button Bears wear boots called Lippos which cling them to their humans. They are very clever, clean bears and always wash and shower when their Flippos do.

Remember, the smaller your belly button, the more likely it is that you will not have a Belly Button Bear because they need room for their tube houses. So you won't have a family of Belly Button Bears living on you until you're grown up.

Old people are treasured, as Belly Button Bears love to explore all the canyons and ravines, trekking over them for days at a time.

Did you hear that whistle? Oh no, I must go before the Belly Button Bear Police catch me, I'm not allowed to tell Flippos about us, it's against the law. I'll find time to tell you about some of the adventures I've been on as soon as I can.

Your friend evermore,
Beeble Belly Button Bear.

New Fiction Information

We hope you have enjoyed reading this book - and that you will continue to enjoy it in the coming years.

If you like reading and writing poetry drop us a line, or give us a call, and we'll send you a free information pack.

Alternatively if you would like to order further copies of this book or any of our other titles, then please give us a call or log onto our website at
www.forwardpress.co.uk

New Fiction Information
Remus House
Coltsfoot Drive
Peterborough
PE2 9JX

(01733) 898101